W9-BID-632

HARLEQUIN®
Presents

Happy New Year from Harlequin Presents! One resolution the editors of Presents like to keep is making time just for themselves by curling up with their favorite books and escaping into a world of glamour, passion and seduction! So why not try this for yourselves, and pick up a Harlequin Presents today?

We've got a great selection for you this month, with THE ROYAL HOUSE OF NIROLI series leading the way. In *Bride by Royal Appointment* by Raye Morgan, Adam must put aside his royal revenge to marry Elena. Then, favorite author Lynne Graham will start your New Year with a bang, with *The Desert Sheikh's Captive Wife,* the first part in her trilogy THE RICH, THE RUTHLESS AND THE REALLY HANDSOME. Jacqueline Baird brings you a brooding Italian seducing his ex-wife in *The Italian Billionaire's Ruthless Revenge,* while in *Bought for Her Baby* by Melanie Milburne, there's a gorgeous Greek claiming a mistress! *The Frenchman's Marriage Demand* by Chantelle Shaw has a sexy millionaire furious that Freya's claiming he has a child, and in *The Virgin's Wedding Night* by Sara Craven, an innocent woman has no choice but to turn to a smoldering Greek for a marriage of convenience. Lee Wilkinson brings you a tycoon holding the key to Sophia's precious secret in *The Padova Pearls,* and, finally, in *The Italian's Chosen Wife* by fantastic new author Kate Hewitt, Italy's most notorious tycoon chooses a waitress to be his bride!

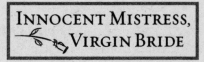

INNOCENT MISTRESS,
VIRGIN BRIDE

Wedded and bedded for the very first time!

Classic romances from your
favorite Presents authors.

Available this month:

The Virgin's Wedding Night
by Sara Craven

Available only from Harlequin Presents®.

Sara Craven

THE VIRGIN'S WEDDING NIGHT

> INNOCENT MISTRESS,
> VIRGIN BRIDE

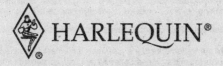

HARLEQUIN®

TORONTO • NEW YORK • LONDON
AMSTERDAM • PARIS • SYDNEY • HAMBURG
STOCKHOLM • ATHENS • TOKYO • MILAN • MADRID
PRAGUE • WARSAW • BUDAPEST • AUCKLAND

ISBN-13: 978-0-373-12696-5
ISBN-10:   0-373-12696-4

THE VIRGIN'S WEDDING NIGHT

First North American Publication 2008.

Copyright © 2007 by Sara Craven.

This edition published by arrangement with Harlequin Books S.A.

® and TM are trademarks of the publisher. Trademarks indicated with
® are registered in the United States Patent and Trademark Office, the
Canadian Trade Marks Office and in other countries.

www.eHarlequin.com

Printed in U.S.A.

All about the author...
Sara Craven

SARA CRAVEN was born in South Devon,
England, and grew up surrounded by books in a
house by the sea. After leaving grammar school she
worked as a local journalist, covering everything
from flower shows to murders. She started writing
for Harlequin in 1975. Sara Craven has appeared
as a contestant on the U.K. Channel Four game
show *Fifteen to One*, and in 1997 won the title of
Television Mastermind of Great Britain.

Sara shares her Somerset home with a West
Highland white terrier called Bertie Wooster,
several thousand books and an amazing video and
DVD collection.

When she's not writing, she likes to travel in
Europe, particularly Greece and Italy. She loves
music, theater, cooking and eating in good
restaurants, but reading will always be her greatest
passion.

Since the birth of her twin grandchildren in New
York City, she has become a regular visitor to the
Big Apple.

CHAPTER ONE

'WHAT do you mean—you can't go through with it?' Harriet Flint stared at the flushed defensive face of the young man on the other side of the table. 'We have an agreement, and this lunch is to finalise the arrangements for the wedding. I'm relying on you.'

'But things have completely changed for me now. You must see that.' His mouth set stubbornly. 'When we made the original deal, frankly I didn't care what happened to me. The girl I loved was out of my life, so the chance of earning a bundle of cash and heading off round the world seemed a fair option.

'But now Janie's come back, and we're together again, for good this time. We're going to be married, and I'm not allowing anything to jeopardise that.'

'But surely if you explained to her…'

'Explain?' Peter Curtis gave a derisive laugh. 'You mean actually tell her that, while we were apart, I agreed to marry some total stranger—for money.'

'Couldn't you make it clear it's not a real marriage—just a temporary arrangement for a few months—and on a strictly business footing. Wouldn't that make a difference?'

'Of course not,' he said impatiently. 'How could it? She'd never accept that I could be involved in something so bizarre. And even if she believed me, she'd think I'd gone stark raving mad, and I wouldn't blame her.'

He shook his head. 'So—I'm sorry, Miss Flint, but the deal's off.

I'm not risking her walking away from me again, because she's all that matters to me. Surely you can understand that.'

'And I have an inheritance that matters to me just as much,' Harriet returned coldly. 'And which I stand to lose if I can't produce a husband before my next birthday. Clearly you've never understood that.'

She paused. 'Consider this. Marriage is an expensive business, these days. I'm sure your Janie realises that. Surely you could persuade her that a tax-free lump sum is worth a small sacrifice, especially if I was able to manage an increase on the original fee.'

'No,' he said. 'She wouldn't see it that way at all. Why should she?' He rose to leave, then paused, looking down at her, frowning a little. 'For God's sake, Miss Flint—Harriet—you don't have to buy a husband. If you wore different clothes—did something to your hair—you could be quite attractive. So, why not tell yourself this was a lucky escape, and concentrate on finding some real happiness instead?'

'Thank you,' she said. 'For the unsolicited advice. But I prefer to do things my way. And that does not involve harnessing my marginal attractions to some man. Not now—not ever. I prefer my career.'

'Well, I can't be the only one who answered your advertisement. Sign up one of the others.'

But you, she thought, were the only one that my grandfather would have believed in as my future husband. You're his idea of the perfect clean-limbed, upstanding young Englishman. Judas Iscariot probably looked like you.

She watched him fumble for his wallet, then shook her head. 'No, I'll pick up the tab, along with the pieces of our agreement. You see, I'd have kept my word, right up to the moment the annulment was validated.

'I hope you always feel you made the right decision,' she added, smiling as he turned to leave. 'And I wish you well.'

It wasn't true, of course. She'd have liked to kill him. Him and his smug bitch of a girlfriend, who only had to crook her little finger, it seemed, to send all Harriet's hopes into chaos.

And what the hell, she asked herself, as she watched him walk away, was she going to do now—with Grandfather's ultimatum on one side, and this—gaping hole on the other?

Well, for this afternoon, at any rate, she would have to relegate her unexpected problem to the back of her mind. She had a tricky meeting, which would require some serious focussing.

She signalled to the waiter, who arrived, his eyes scanning her untouched plate of *penne arrabiata* with open distress.

'There is something wrong with the food, *signorina?*'

'Not at all,' she assured him. 'I—wasn't very hungry, that's all.' *Something killed my appetite stone-dead.*

'Quite attractive,' she thought, smouldering. And then shook her head. How condescending was it possible to get?

She supposed that, in looks, she must take after her unknown father. Her hair was undoubtedly her best feature, brown as a horse-chestnut with auburn lights. And, if she'd permitted it to do so, it would have hung waving to her shoulders. Her eyes were clear and grey, and thickly lashed, but the rest of her face was totally unremarkable. So—if this had been Dad—what on earth had the blonde and ravishing Caroline Flint seen in such a man—unless, of course, he'd had oodles of charm.

If so, I missed out twice, Harriet thought cynically.

Not that she allowed it to trouble her. She had no wish to resemble her mother in either looks or temperament, so she'd been deeply riled by her grandfather's on-going assumption that she couldn't wait to kick over the traces and bring a double helping of dishonour on the family name.

Unlike Caroline Flint, she'd never shown the least inclination to indulge in a welter of short-lived and very public affairs with any man who took her fancy, married or single.

Not, she had to admit, that the opportunity had ever presented itself. She'd done a little perfunctory dating when she'd first arrived in London, but none of those encounters had ever developed as far as a full-blown relationship. Nor had she wanted it to happen. And recently there'd been nothing. Which was fine by her too.

She rose, suddenly impatient to be off, picking up her bag, and slinging the jacket of her dull black linen suit over her arm as she made her way across the restaurant to the desk at the front where Luigi the owner held sway.

Only, he was already occupied with a tall young man who'd just walked in off the street, while Harriet had been negotiating her passage between the crowded tables. And the street looked as if it was the place where he belonged, Harriet thought, resenting that she was being forced to wait in line. And by someone like this too.

Because torn jeans, worn-out trainers and a much faded tee shirt were hardly the fashion choices of Luigi's usual male clientele. And the over-long, untidy dark hair, and thin, unshaven face hardly struck a reassuring note either.

In fact, by now, Harriet would have expected the newcomer to have been ushered politely but firmly to the door.

Only it wasn't happening. In fact Luigi was all smiles and amiability and—dear God—actually reaching for his chequebook.

Paying him to go away? Harriet wondered with wry bewilderment. Luigi ran an excellent restaurant, but she'd never gained the impression before that he was a soft touch. Unless there was some more sinister implication to the visit, and the stranger was collecting for some kind of protection racket.

Her mouth twisted in swift self-derision. Don't let your imagination gallop away with you, my dear, she adjured herself.

Besides, people like that probably don't take cheques anyway.

While this particular payment was being accepted with alacrity, she noticed, and transferred to the shabby wallet taken from the back pocket of those terminally scruffy jeans.

A few quick words, a handshake, and then he was turning to go. For a moment Harriet found herself facing him, confusedly aware that, in spite of his outward dishevelment, which gave the disturbing impression that he'd just fallen out of bed and grabbed the first handful of clothing he saw, his face was cool and contained, the nose high-bridged, the mouth firm above a square chin. That, if not handsome, he was certainly—striking—maybe even downright attractive, his shoulders broad, and his body lean and muscular.

She was conscious too of his eyes, dark as a night sky, encountering her glance in turn, and brushing over her with total indifference as he went, and the restaurant door closed behind him.

For a moment, she felt oddly shaken, her hand going up almost defensively to smooth the collar of her white cotton shirt.

As if, she thought, it mattered what she looked like. As if she didn't deliberately dress down every day of her life, wearing deliberately dull clothing, and dragging her hair relentlessly back from her face to be confined at the nape of her neck by an elastic band. Because, with her mother's example never far from her mind, she was the last person in the world to want to attract a man's attention or interest.

Especially one who looked like that, she thought tartly, pulling herself together and retrieving her credit card from her bag.

But Luigi's good humour seemed to be universal today, and he waved away the proffered payment.

'You ate nothing, Miss Flint, and you drank only water. Your friend did little better. I hope, on your next visit, you will have better appetites.'

By my next visit, I may well have lost my entire inheritance, Harriet thought bitterly, as she forced a grateful smile. And the friend in question will not be with me.

As she turned to go, Luigi halted her, his voice sinking confidentially. 'That man who was just here—you observed him, I think, and must have wondered.'

To her annoyance, she felt herself flush. 'It's really none of my business…'

'No, no, this will interest you, because you were the first to notice the picture and admire it.' He gestured expansively at the expanse of pale lemon wall behind him. 'I should have told him so.'

'Told him?' Harriet repeated slowly. She looked up at the framed canvas which had been hanging there for the past three weeks, and her brows snapped together in amazement. 'You mean—*he* painted *that*?'

'*Si.*' Luigi nodded, his mouth quirking in amusement. 'He looks the part, no? The struggling artist in his garret?' Luigi shrugged. 'Yet, he has talent. You yourself said so, *signorina.*'

Harriet looked back at the painting. It was all perfectly true, she acknowledged with silent reluctance. It had captured her attention, and her imagination, from the first moment she'd seen it. Yet it wasn't the kind of thing that usually appealed to her.

At first glance, it was a relatively simple composition—clearly some Mediterranean scene with a cloudless sky above a crescent of beach, with the blue haze of the sea beyond. In the foreground was a small plateau of bleached and barren rock, flat and featureless, and on it was a table holding a half-empty bottle of wine and two glasses, one of which had overturned, sending a small trickle of liquid, rusty as dried blood, across the white metal surface. Just under the rock, half buried in the sand, was a woman's discarded sandal, a fragile high-heeled thing. Nothing more.

It was a picture that asked questions—that invited speculation—but that hadn't been its main appeal for Harriet. Then, as now, the heavy golden light that suffused it, burning and languid, had made her feel as if she was looking into the very essence of heat. That she could feel it searing her eyes, and scorching her skin, even through her layers of clothing.

And that was what had alerted her to the skill of the painter—what lifted the picture to a different dimension.

When she'd questioned Luigi initially, he'd shrugged and said it was an experiment. That he was featuring it to gauge the reaction of his customers.

And she'd looked back at it again, and said slowly, 'I think—in fact I'm sure that it's good—and that I like it very much.' Adding, 'If that means anything.'

Certainly it was as far removed from the rather conventional watercolour of Positano that had hung there before as it was possible to get.

At the same time, Harriet was aware that she'd always found the picture strangely disturbing. That, as well as the faint mystery of its subject matter, it seemed, in some way, to emanate an anger as tangible as the scrape of a fingernail on flesh.

Nevertheless, her eyes were instinctively drawn to it each time she came to the restaurant, and she invariably lingered for an extra moment at the desk to study it.

Now, on a sudden, inexplicable impulse, she said, 'Is it for sale?'

He looked remorseful. 'I regret—it has already gone. But he has other, very different work for which he wishes to find a market, and

I have been able to send interested buyers to him. Also he accepts commissions.'

He paused. 'But what he needs, *signorina*, is a patron—someone with contacts in the art world—an exhibition in a gallery to make him known.'

He delved under the desk and handed her a cheaply printed business card. It carried the single word 'Roan', and a mobile telephone number.

She studied it, wondering whether Roan was a given name or a surname. 'Pretty basic.'

'It is not easy when you are at the beginning of your career.'

'I suppose not.' She slipped the card into a side pocket of her bag, intending to dispose of it later. Asking about the picture had been a pure whim, coming at her from nowhere, and best forgotten.

Besides, right now she had her own struggles to contend with, she thought as she walked out into the sunlit street. And this state of deadlock with her grandfather was set fair and square centre-stage.

Harriet smothered a sigh as she began to walk briskly back to her office. She loved Grandfather—of course she did—and she owed him a hell of a lot, but she was under no illusions about him either.

Gregory Flint was a total flesh-eating, swamp-bound dinosaur. Tyrannosaurus Rex, alive and in person. He always had been, and he certainly saw no reason to change—not at his time of life, nor in his current state of health.

And, however preposterous his demands, it was unwise to shrug them off and hope he would forget, as she was now discovering to her cost.

She could only imagine the scene when her mother, eighteen and unwed, had defiantly announced that she was pregnant, that marriage to the father was out of the question, and that she would never agree to a termination. Could imagine too that the subsequent explosion would have rocked the Richter scale.

Certainly the news had created a breach that had caused Caroline Flint to be barred from the family home, especially when she'd refused to atone for her sins by giving the baby up for adoption. And it had been six years before contact was resumed.

'Your grandfather wants to see you, darling,' her mother had announced lightly one day. 'Which means that the prodigal daughter is being given a second chance too. Wonders will never cease.'

Her partner at the time, an unemployed session guitarist called Bryn, had glanced up at her. 'Don't knock it, Princess. We could use a fatted calf.'

They went down to Gracemead the following day, and as the station taxi turned the corner in the drive, and the house lay in front of them, Harriet drew a breath of stunned, incredulous joy. Because it didn't seem possible after the cheap flats she was used to that she could be even marginally connected with such a truly magical place.

In time, she'd come to see that Gracemead was not really beautiful. That her Flint ancestor, the wealthy Victorian merchant who'd taken a classic Georgian house and embellished it with a Gothic façade, before adding turrets at each end in imitation of his sovereign's Scottish retreat at Balmoral, had actually been something of a vandal.

But, seeing it that first time as a confused and not always happy child, she gasped in wonder as the afternoon sun touched the windows, and flecked the stones with gold, telling herself it was a fairy palace, and that her mother must genuinely be the Princess that Bryn called her to have been born there.

The interview between Gregory Flint and his errant daughter was conducted in private. Harriet was whisked off to the kitchen by a plump, elderly woman who'd been Caroline's old nanny, and plied with milk and small iced cakes with smiley faces that had been piped on to them by Mrs Wade, the cook-housekeeper.

When she eventually joined them, her mother was smiling too, but with a kind of rigid determination, and her eyes were red.

'Such fun, sweetie. You're going to stay here with Grandpa and have a wonderful time. Spoiled to death, I expect, don't you, Nanny?'

'Aren't you staying too?' Harriet asked in bewilderment, but Caroline shook her head.

'I'll be going with Bryn, darling. He has a marvellous tour of America coming up with a very famous singer. We'll be away for ages, so it's best that you're here. It's a wonderful place to grow up in,' she added, the lovely face momentarily shadowed with something like regret.

And so it had proved, thought Harriet. Because she'd never actually lived with her mother again after that, seeing her only from time to time as someone whose visits became less and less frequent.

The house had become the constant in her life—had become her home. And that initial sense of wonder—almost of recognition—had never faded. She'd felt from the start that the place was reaching out to her to hug her—to soothe away any sense of abandonment she might feel. And she'd hugged it back, knowing that it was where she truly belonged.

Accustomed to London's restrictions, she'd found Gracemead and its large grounds had provided her with a magical playground to explore for hours at a time. And Nanny and Mrs Wade had almost vied with each other to make sure she lacked for nothing to make her feel comfortable and secure.

Her relationship with her grandfather had taken rather longer to establish. He'd been awkward with her at first, taciturn and more than a little gruff. And sometimes she'd found him watching her as if he was puzzled about something. Then, one day, she'd heard one of the local ladies refer to her as 'Poor Caroline's little girl. You would never know, would you?' and understood.

It was the day he'd found her in his book-lined study, deep in *Black Beauty*, twining a strand of hair round her finger as she read, that everything had changed between them.

She hadn't realised immediately that she was no longer alone, and when she'd looked up and seen him watching her, she'd been apprehensive in case he was angry.

But his sudden smile had been strangely tender. 'Your mother used to do that when she was reading,' he told her. 'And this was her favourite book too.'

He sat down in the big wing chair by the fireplace and began to talk to her, listening patiently to her halting replies, and encouraging her to be less shy, and say whatever was on her mind.

Looking back, Harriet could even say with honesty that she'd had a pretty good childhood in spite of her mother's continuing and prolonged absences. There'd been postcards at first, and letters from the States, then from Europe, after the relationship with Bryn had finally crashed and burned like all the others, and Caroline had joined up with a professional tennis player, not quite in the top rank.

Eventually, as the years had passed, the letters had become fewer, then dried up altogether. At the last contact—a card for her twenty-first birthday—Caroline had seemed to be in Argentina living with a former polo player. But no address had been included, and since then there'd been nothing to indicate whether her mother was alive or dead.

Harriet had come to accept over the years that her mother lived solely on her own terms, and that the existence of her child belonged to a long-discarded past. She was left to remember only Caroline's beauty and zest for life, however misplaced, and to try and forget the negative elements of their relationship. At the same time, however, her life with her grandfather, though never lacking in affection, grew marginally trickier.

Gregory Flint was clearly determined that Harriet was not going to follow in her mother's footsteps if there was anything he could do to prevent it. Accordingly, Harriet found her life controlled by a kind of benevolent despotism, her freedom restricted and her judgement regularly called into question.

And the fact that she could—almost—understand why it was happening made it no less irksome.

The first major clash between them had come when she was eighteen, and had just left her convent school, and he'd announced he'd found her a place in a Swiss establishment where she would improve her foreign language skills, and embark on a *cordon bleu* cookery course.

She'd stared at him open-mouthed: 'You mean I'm going to be *finished*? Gramps, you can't mean it. Anyone would think we were living a hundred years ago.'

His brows snapped together. 'You have some other idea?'

'Well, of course.' She tried her most winning smile. 'I've decided to join the family business. Carry on the Flint name for another generation.'

'You—want to work for Flint Audley?' He gave a harsh laugh. 'And where did this ridiculous notion spring from, I wonder?'

'It seems an obvious choice,' she countered.

'Well, it's not obvious to me,' he said scathingly. 'What on earth do you think you know about property management on the scale we deal with? Dealing with our range of tenants, contracts, maintenance—the thousand and one issues you'd be faced with? You—a chit of a girl just out of school?'

'I'd know about as much as you and Gordon Audley did when you started out in the fifties.' Harriet lifted her chin without flinching. 'And certainly as much as Jonathan Audley with his 2:2 in Fine Arts,' she added, her tone edged. 'Yet he seems to have been welcomed with open arms—even by you. I could run rings round him, given the chance.'

She paused. 'Because I'm not just "a chit of a girl" as you claim. I'm a chip off the old block, and all I want is an opportunity to prove myself.' She added more quietly. 'I—I thought you'd be pleased.'

'Then you can think again, and quickly too.' His voice was cutting. 'I have very different plans for your future, my girl.'

'Yes, I know. Polite French conversation halfway up some Alp.' She shook her head. 'Gramps, darling, it would never work. I'd be so *bored*. And you know what they say about idle hands,' she added unthinkingly, and saw his face harden into real anger.

'Is that a reference to your mother?'

She bit her lip. 'No, I promise it's not.' *Although maybe things might have turned out differently for her if she'd been allowed to have a real job—a career from the outset—instead of being expected to stay at home, the dutiful daughter. Perhaps that original love affair was her first chance to be herself. To make a choice, even if it was the wrong one...*

She thought it, but did not say it. Instead, she went on coaxingly, 'All the same, I'd like to pass on the social graces, and start earning my living like everyone else I know.'

There was a silence, then he said, 'Well, there's no need to be in too much of a hurry to decide about the future. Why not take one of those gap years, and spend some time at home, while you make up your mind? If you need an occupation, there's always plenty of voluntary work about.'

'Gramps, my mind is made up.' She took a deep breath. 'And Larry Brotherton is interviewing me for a job as an assistant in the rents review department on Monday.'

'No one,' her grandfather said ominously, 'has seen fit to mention this to me. And I am still nominally supposed to be the chairman of the board.'

'With your mind, presumably, on higher things than the recruitment of very junior staff.' She shrugged. 'Anyway, Mr Brotherton may turn me down.'

'I doubt that very much.' He was silent for a moment, then grunted. 'I suppose if you're determined I can't stop you. And Flint Audley will do as well as anywhere—until, of course, you're ready to settle down.'

And I laughed, and said, 'Of course,' thought Harriet.

She'd been too pleased with her victory to consider the clear implication in his words. That working at Flint Audley would be merely a stop-gap arrangement until she fulfilled her female destiny by making a sensible marriage.

And when, to her delight, she'd been offered the job, she'd thrown herself into it, working so conspicuously hard that promotion had soon followed. Now, six years later, driven by ambition and hard graft, she was at management level, with a salary to match, a generous bonus, and a possible brief to expand the commercial management branch of the company outside London.

That was if the afternoon's meeting went her way, as she was determined that it should.

Her colleagues might not like her particularly—she knew that behind her back she was called 'Harriet the Harridan'—but they couldn't knock her achievements, and that was what she cared about.

If only Gramps could have been equally satisfied, she thought bitterly. But there'd never been any chance of that. His opinion of her career had remained totally unchanged—that it was simply a way of keeping busy until real life intervened, and she found herself a suitable man.

But over the past year his attitude had hardened to the point of disaster.

'Gracemead is a house for a family, not a single woman,' he'd growled. 'You've wasted enough time, my girl. Find yourself a decent man and bring him home as your husband, or I'll change my will. Arrange for the place to be sold after I'm gone.'

She'd stared at him open-mouthed. 'Gramps—you're not serious. You can't be.'

'I mean every word,' he'd returned ominously. 'I'm going to set you a deadline, Harriet. If you're not engaged, or better still married, by your next birthday, I shall contact my lawyers. As my heiress, you'd be vulnerable—prey to any smooth-talking crook who came along. I intend to see you with a strong man at your side.'

'I don't believe this.' She'd been breathless with shock and anger. 'That kind of thinking belongs in the Ark.'

He'd nodded grimly. 'And everything in the Ark went in two by two—exactly as nature intended. And if you want this house, you'll do the same.'

Remembering, Harriet caught a glimpse of herself in a shop window, scowling ferociously, and hastily rearranged her expression into more agreeable lines. She made it a strict rule never to take any personal problems into the office, so no one knew about the rock and the hard place currently confronting her in her private life.

'And they're not going to know, either,' she muttered under her breath. This afternoon she had to make a conscious effort to win hearts and minds for her expansion programme, and she already knew that her plans would be under attack by Jonathan Audley, just for the sake of it.

He'd been furious when she'd first overtaken him in the promotion stakes, and she knew she had him to thank for her less than flattering nickname.

But then he's never heard what I call him under my breath, she thought.

All the same, there were times when she wanted to take hold of him by his pure silk designer tie, and say, Look, we're on the same side, you pathetic idiot. Stop being a total obstruction.

But it wasn't just office politics. Harriet knew that she'd offended Jonathan's male ego long ago, by signally failing to appreciate the charms that had set the young secretaries in a dither since he'd joined the company.

Too pleased with himself by half had been her original thinking, and she'd seen no reason to alter her opinion since. Except, maybe, to add 'bloody nuisance' to his list of failings.

And today, unfortunately, she would need every scrap of patience she possessed in order to deal with him.

As she rounded the corner into the square where Flint Audley's offices were located, she saw that a group of people had gathered outside the small railed garden opposite the building, and were watching something intently.

Curious, Harriet slowed a little, wondering what had attracted their attention. If there'd been some kind of accident, which might require emergency action.

Then, as realisation dawned, her brows snapped together. Good God, she thought. It's the guy from the restaurant—the alley-cat artist.

Sitting sideways on the low wall, one long leg tucked under him and a board balanced on his lap, he was sketching rapidly.

As Harriet watched, he tore off the sheet of paper he'd been working on, and handed it with a bow to the girl directly in front of him, amid laughter and applause from the others standing around.

Not just vaguely sinister Mediterranean scenes, this time around, but instant portraits, it seemed. Was this the other—different—work that Luigi had mentioned? She was aware of an odd disappointment as the subject of the sketch blushed, giggled, then bent, a little awkwardly, to put some money in the box at his feet.

Well, that certainly confirmed what Luigi had also said about him being hard up, she thought.

Not that she could allow it to make a difference.

The square was a pretty exclusive location, and besides, he probably needed a licence for what he was doing, and she'd bet good money he didn't have one.

And then, just as if he'd picked up her thought-waves across the width of the road, he looked at her, the dark brows lifting in recognition. Only this time he didn't look away, subjecting her to a long, searching look that rested on her face, then travelled with lingering arrogance the entire length of her body, as if he was asking some silent question.

There was something in his gaze that caught Harriet completely on the raw, prompting—and deepening—the feelings of self-consciousness she'd experienced at their earlier encounter. Something which she could not understand, and certainly didn't appreciate.

You're one step away from down-and-out, my friend, she addressed him silently. So, talented or not, you're in no real position to issue any kind of challenge, as you're about to find out.

She turned and swept into the building.

'Les,' she said to the security man behind the reception desk. 'Get that person across the road to move on, will you?' She forced a smile. 'He's making the place look untidy.'

He gave her a surprised look. 'Not doing any real harm is he, miss?'

'Apart from causing an obstruction,' Harriet said crisply. 'Anyway, I'd prefer not to discuss it.'

She walked to the lift, aware that a cloud of disapproval was following her.

But I can't afford to care about that now, she told herself, as she rode upwards. So, Luigi's tame artist can just push off and struggle somewhere else. And good riddance to him.

And, gritting her teeth, she marched out of the lift, off to do battle over something that really mattered.

CHAPTER TWO

'WELL, you were a great deal of help,' Tony Morton, Harriet's immediate boss commented sourly as they left the meeting. 'What the hell was wrong with you? This expansion on the commercial side is supposed to be your pet project, and yet half the time you seemed to be in a trance.'

He gave her a frowning look. 'So, what is it? Have you fallen in love?'

Harriet gasped. 'No,' she said. 'No, of course not.'

'Well, something must be going on,' he said moodily. He threw his arms in the air. 'My God, when you were talking about that development site in the Midlands, you actually said "beachside" instead of "canalside". What was that about?'

'I was probably thinking of the canal's leisure and holiday opportunities,' was the only lame excuse Harriet could come up with on the spur of the moment. 'It was a slip of the tongue,' she added, cursing under her breath.

A Freudian slip, more like, she admitted silently. It had been hot in the boardroom, and that damned picture from the restaurant had kept coming back into her mind. For a moment there she'd imagined she actually felt the relentless beat of the sun, and the burn of the sand under her bare feet. But that wasn't all.

For some unfathomable reason, the man Roan's dark face had suddenly intruded into her consciousness too, the shadowed eyes glinting as if in mockery. Or even, she thought, scorn.

And that was the moment she'd found herself floundering…

Which was, she told herself, totally absurd.

'Well, you can't afford any more of these slips.' Tony shook his head. 'Now we have a three-month delay while we prepare yet another report. The whole scheme has lost whatever priority status it had. Unbelievable.'

Harriet bit her lip. 'Tony, I'm really sorry. Naturally, I realised it wasn't going to be a walkover, but it isn't a total defeat either.'

'We were let off the hook, sweetheart,' he reminded her grimly. 'I only hope that next time you'll have got your beans in a row as efficiently as Jonathan marshalled the opposition today.'

Well, she couldn't argue about that, Harriet thought, mortified. She'd been well and truly ambushed. She'd expected the usual clash of horns, and encountered instead a 'more in sorrow than in anger' routine from Jonathan, which accused her elliptically of trying to split the company and establish her own independent business empire.

Caught on the back foot, she'd rallied and offered a vehement denial, but not quickly enough, and she could tell that the seed had been sown in the minds around the table, and that alarm bells were ringing.

And while Flint Audley commanded her total loyalty, she had to admit the chance of escaping from the hothouse politicking of the London office for a while had seemed deeply attractive.

'It would also be a good thing,' Tony said, pausing with a frown in the doorway of his office, 'if you'd resolve this ridiculous feud with Jon Audley. It's doing no good at all.'

Harriet gasped. 'You're blaming me for it?'

'Not blaming,' he said. 'Just noting that he seems to command more support round here than you do at the moment. And today he sounded like the voice of sweet reason, not you.' He paused. 'Maybe you should bear that in mind when you're preparing your analysis of what went wrong earlier. I'd like it on my desk tomorrow.'

Going into her own room, Harriet managed to resist the temptation to slam the door hard.

Tony's last comments might be unfair, she thought furiously, but there was little she could say in her own defence about the way things had gone. She had not given the job in hand her usual un-flinching concentration, and she knew it. What she could not explain to herself was—why?

Because it wasn't just the commercial project that was slipping away from her, but her entire life. And somehow she had to get it back. All of it.

She took a step towards her desk, then stopped. Oh, to hell with it, she thought impatiently, glancing at her watch. Pointless to imagine I can achieve anything useful for the rest of the afternoon, when my mind's flying off in all directions like this. Besides, I was in before eight this morning. I'm going home.

It occurred to her that, apart from anything else, she was hungry. A shower and a meal might make her feel more inclined to reprise the events of the meeting, and pinpoint what positive aspects there'd been.

At the moment, she couldn't think of any, but she would never admit as much. This is just a glitch, she told herself firmly. I'll bounce back. If only I didn't have so much else on my plate.

She squared her shoulders, then picked up her bag, and the shoulder case with her laptop, and headed for the door.

She was halfway down the corridor when she heard a burst of laughter coming from the office she was approaching, and recog-nised Jonathan's voice.

'I suppose I should feel guilty for knocking Flinty's baby on the head,' he was saying. 'Especially as it's the only time hell's spinster is ever likely to give birth—to anything. Not even all Grandpa's money would be enough to tempt a sane man to take her on. But, try as I may, I can't manage one single regret. I truly feel she'd be happier in a back office, working the photocopier.'

'You mean you'd be happier if that's where she was,' Anthea, his assistant, said over another sycophantic ripple of amusement. It sounded as if quite a crowd had gathered.

'Infinitely,' Jonathan drawled. 'Maybe we should try it. Offer her a title—vice-president in charge of paperclips—and see what happens. After all, she's only playing at a career. Old Gregory made that clear from the first,' he added with a snap. 'I bet he can't believe she's still here. And I can tell you that Tony's well and truly sick of being saddled with her.'

Harriet stood where she was, lips parted in shock. This was more than the idle malice of the nicknames, she realised numbly. There was genuine entrenched resentment here. Jonathan Audley wanted her out, and it seemed he was not alone in that.

So, today wasn't just a skirmish. It was the opening salvo in a war she hadn't realised had been declared. And it had clearly hit the target.

Her hand tightened on the handle of her briefcase. She lifted her chin, then walked forward, halting at the half-open door. Standing there as the amusement faded into embarrassed silence. Glancing round as if she was taking note of who was there—collating names and faces—before walking on down the corridor, her head high.

But her hand was shaking as she pressed the button to summon the lift. Behind her, she heard a burst of nervous giggling, and Jon Audley's voice saying, 'Oops.' A sixth sense told her that someone had come out into the corridor and was watching her, waiting, probably, for some other reaction, so she made herself lean a casual shoulder against the wall, glancing idly at her watch while she waited.

Thankfully, the lift was empty, and as the door closed she sank down on to her haunches, trying to steady her uneven breathing, fighting off the astonishing threat of tears, because she never cried.

By the time the ground floor was reached, she'd got herself back under control, and she'd at least be able to leave the building in good order.

Home, she thought longingly. My own space. My own things. A chance to regroup.

As she crossed the reception area, Les called to her. 'That artist bloke has gone, Miss Flint, like you wanted.'

She swung round, confronting him almost dazedly, wondering what he was talking about. When she finally remembered, it was as if the incident had occurred in another lifetime.

She said curtly, 'Good. I hope he didn't give you any trouble.'

'Not a bit, miss.' He hesitated. 'In fact he seemed a bit amused when I approached him. As if he'd been expecting it.' He paused again. 'And later, when I went out to check that he'd gone, I found this, fastened to the railings outside.'

He reached into a drawer, and with clear embarrassment handed her a sheet of cartridge paper, folded in half.

Harriet opened it out, and found herself looking at what seemed to be a mass of black shading. For a brief instant, she thought it must be a drawing of a bat—or a bird of prey. A carrion crow, perhaps, with wings spread wide, about to swoop.

And then she saw the face emerging from those dark flying draperies. A woman's face—sullen—angry—driven. A caricature, perhaps, portrayed without subtlety, but, she realised, unmistakably—unforgivably—her face.

A deliberate and calculated insult—signed 'Roan' across one corner with such force that it had almost torn the paper.

For a long moment, she stared down at the drawing in silence. Then she forced a smile.

'Quite a work of art.' Somehow, she managed to keep her voice light. 'Everything but the broomstick. And—fastened to the railings, you say? For all the world to see?'

Les nodded unhappily, his ruddy face deepening in colour.

'Afraid so, miss, but it can't have been there long. And no one from here will have spotted it.' he added, as if this was some kind of consolation.

'I think you mean no one else,' she said quietly. She folded the paper, and put it carefully in her briefcase.

'Are you sure you want to do that, miss?' His voice was uncertain. 'You wouldn't like me to put it through the shredder?'

I'd like you to put him—*this Roan*—through the shredder, Harriet wanted to scream. Followed by Tony, and bloody, *bloody* Jonathan. And every other man who dares to judge me. Or force me into some mould of their making like Grandfather.

Instead, she shrugged a shoulder, feigning insouciance, although pain and anger were twisting inside her. 'I intend to treasure it. Who knows? It might be worth a lot of money some day. He may turn out to be a future Hogarth. Besides, isn't it supposed to be salutary to see ourselves as others do?'

Les's face was dubious. 'If you say so, Miss Flint.'

'However,' she added, 'if I send you out to shift any more vagabonds, I give you full permission to ignore my instructions.'

She flashed a last bright, meaningless smile at him, and went out into the street, signalling to a passing taxi.

She gave her home address automatically, and sank back in the corner of the seat, staring unseeingly out of the window, feeling her heart pounding against her ribcage as her anger grew. As the whole day emptied its bitterness into her mind. Culminating in this—this last piece of ignominy perpetrated by a total stranger.

What the hell am I? she asked herself. Punch-bag of the week?

Mouth tightening ominously, she took out her mobile phone and punched in a number.

'Luigi? Harriet Flint.' She spoke evenly. 'The painter. Do you know where he lives? If he has a studio?'

'Of course. One moment.'

He sounded so pleased that Harriet felt almost sorry. Almost, but not quite.

She wrote the directions on the back of the card he'd given her earlier. When I thought things couldn't possibly get any worse, she thought, as she tapped on the glass and told the cabdriver about the change of plan.

She would deal with Jonathan and co in her own good time, she thought as she sat back. But this so-called artist would answer now for his attempt to denigrate her.

Because, but for Les, this drawing would have been seen by the entire company on their way out of the building.

And she knew that it would not have been an easy thing to live down. That it was something that would have lingered on in the corporate memory to be sniggered over as long as she was associated with Flint Audley—which basically meant the rest of her working life.

Just as if she didn't have enough problems already.

She took one last look at the drawing, then closed her fist around it, scrunching it into a ball.

Meanwhile, the cab was slowing. 'This is it, miss,' the driver threw over his shoulder. 'Hildon Yard.'

And home, it seemed, to a flourishing road haulage company, and a row of storage units. Not exactly an artistic environment, she thought, her mouth twisting.

'Will you wait, please?' she requested as she paid the driver. 'I shouldn't be longer than ten minutes,' she added quickly, seeing his reluctant expression.

He nodded resignedly. 'Ten minutes it is,' he said, reaching for his newspaper. 'But that's it.'

Harriet glanced around her, then, after a moment's hesitation, approached a man in brown overalls moving around the trucks with a clipboard, and a preoccupied expression.

She said, 'Can you help me, please? I'm looking for number 6a.'

He pointed unsmilingly to an iron staircase in one corner. 'Up at the top there. That green door.'

Her heels rang on the metal steps as she climbed. Like the clash of armour before battle, she thought, and found she was unexpectedly fighting a very real temptation to forget the whole thing, return to the waiting cab, and go home.

But that was the coward's way out, she told herself. And that arrogant bastard wasn't getting away with what he'd tried to do to her.

As she reached the narrow platform at the top, the door opened suddenly, and Harriet took an involuntary step backwards, pressing herself against the guard rail.

A girl's voice with a smile in it said, 'See you later,' and she found herself confronting a pretty girl, immaculate in pastel cut-offs and a white tee shirt, her blonde hair in a long braid, carrying a large canvas bag slung over one shoulder. She checked, with a gasp, when she spotted Harriet.

'Heavens, you startled me.' Blue eyes looked her over enquiringly. 'Was there something you wanted?'

Harriet saw that the hand holding the strap of the canvas bag wore a wedding ring. The possibility that this Roan might be married had not, frankly, occurred to her.

But, even if he was, there was no way someone so irredeemably scruffy could possibly be paired with a such a clearly high-maintenance woman.

Unless the attraction of opposites had come into play, and he was her bit of rough, she thought with distaste.

The girl said more insistently, 'Can I help you?'

Discovering that she seemed to have momentarily lost the power of speech, Harriet mutely held out the business card that she was still clutching.

'Oh.' The girl sounded surprised. 'Oh—right.' She turned and called over her shoulder, 'Darling, you have a visitor.' She gave Harriet a smile that was friendly and puzzled in equal measures, then clattered her way down the staircase.

Darling...

My God, Harriet thought, wincing. Lady, you have all my sympathy.

At the same time, she was glad the other girl had departed, because what she wanted to say, possibly at the top of her voice, didn't need an audience. Especially when the evidence suggested she could not count on its support.

She drew a deep, steadying breath, took the screwed-up drawing from her pocket, and walked through the doorway.

Because of its immediate environment, she'd expected the place to be dark inside, and probably dingy. Instead she found herself in a large loft room, brimming with the sunlight that poured through the vast window occupying the greater part of an entire wall, and down from the additional skylights in the roof.

The smell of oil paint was thick and heavy in the air, and on the edge of her half-dazzled vision, stacked round the walls, were canvases—great splashes of vibrant, singing colour.

But she couldn't allow them to distract her, even for a moment, because *he* was there—a tall, dark figure, standing motionless, hands on hips, in the middle of all this brilliance.

As if he was waiting for her, hard and unbending as a granite pillar, the black brows drawn together in a frown, his mouth harsh and unsmiling.

He said, 'What are you doing here? What do you want?'

His voice was low-pitched and cool. Educated too, she recognised with faint surprise, but slightly accented. Spanish—Italian? She couldn't be sure.

Of course that deep tan should have given away his Mediterranean origins, as she now had every opportunity to notice, because the tee shirt he'd been wearing earlier had been discarded. His feet were bare too, and the waistband of his jeans, worn low on his hips, was unfastened.

As it would be, she thought, if he'd simply dragged them on for decency's sake as he said goodbye to his lover.

And, while there wasn't an ounce of spare flesh on him, effete he certainly wasn't, she realised, swallowing. His naked shoulders and arms were powerfully sculpted, and his bronzed chest was darkly shadowed by the hair that arrowed down over his stomach until hidden by the barrier of faded denim that covered his long legs.

Penniless artist he might be, but at the same time he looked tough and uncompromising, and it occurred to her suddenly that perhaps it might have been better if the blonde had remained after all.

Or if I'd stayed away...

The thoughts seemed to be chasing each other through her skull.

'I asked why you were here,' he said. 'And I am waiting for your answer.'

That jolted her back to the here and now. Needled her into response too.

She lifted her chin. 'Can't you guess the reason?' She took the crumpled ball of paper from her pocket, and threw it at him. It didn't reach its target, dropping harmlessly to the floor between them, and he didn't waste a glance on it.

'You were so impressed with the likeness that you came to commission a portrait, perhaps?' His tone was silky. 'If so, I must refuse. I doubt if I could summon up sufficient inspiration a second time.'

'Don't worry.' Her own voice grated. 'I have no plans to feature as a subject for you ever again. I came for an apology.'

His brows lifted. 'An apology for what?'

'For *that*.' She pointed at the ball of paper. 'That—thing you left for me.' She drew a swift, sharp breath. 'Do you know how many people work in that building—and use that entrance? And you had the damned nerve to put that—insulting, libellous daub where everyone would see it. Make me into a laughing stock. And you did it quite deliberately. Don't try to deny it.'

He shrugged. 'Why should I?'

'And don't pretend it was only a joke, either. Because, if so, it was in bloody poor taste.'

'It was no joke,' he said, and there was a note in his voice that gave her the odd sensation that her skin had been laid open by a whip. 'And nor was your attempt to have me moved on by your security guard, as if I was guilty of some crime. And in front of a crowd of people, too.

'Humiliation does not appeal to me either,' he added grimly. 'Although I must tell you that your plan misfired, because no one laughed. They were all embarrassed for me, including your guard. And several of them sprang to my defence.'

He paused. 'It is interesting that you did not expect your colleagues to be equally supportive,' he went on bitingly. 'But, at the same time, it is hardly surprising if this is a sample of the tactics you use in your workplace. Perhaps they would have recognised my portrait of you only too well.'

She felt as if she'd been punched in the guts, and, for a moment, she could only stare at him in silence. Then, she forced herself to rally. To fight back. 'You had no right to be there, opposite our offices.'

'I have been sketching there all week,' he said. 'No one from your company or any other has complained before.'

'That,' she said, 'is because I never saw you there before.'

'Then I can be thankful for that, at least.'

She bit her lip. 'Anyway, beggars deserve to be moved on. You were causing an obstruction.'

'I was not begging,' he said stonily. 'I was earning honest money, giving pleasure by my sketching. But I guess that pleasure is not something you would readily understand, Miss Harriet Flint.'

She gasped. 'How do you know my name?'

He shrugged. 'In the same way that you learned where I live. I was told by Luigi Carossa. He telephoned to say you were planning to pay me a visit.' His mouth curled. 'He even thought it might be to my advantage. I did not disillusion him.'

He paused. 'Now, if there is nothing further, perhaps you would leave.'

It was difficult to breathe. 'Is that—is that all you have to say?'

'Why, no.' The dark eyes swept over her contemptuously. 'There is also this. Go back to your fortress, Miss Flint, and practise giving more ridiculous and high-handed orders. If you cannot make yourself liked, you can at least attempt to feel important. I hope it is some consolation.'

He kicked the ball of paper towards her. 'And take this with you as a reminder not to over-reach yourself again. This time you escaped lightly, but next time you may indeed find yourself the office joke.'

The world seemed to slip away from her. 'Lightly?' she repeated dazedly. Then, her voice rising, 'You said—lightly?'

She didn't lose her temper as a rule. She had too many bad memories from early childhood of voices shouting, the sound of things being thrown, even occasional blows, and her mother's loud, hysterical weeping as yet another relationship bit the dust.

She'd always prided herself on being able to control her anger. To hide any negative emotions and deal with them calmly and sensibly.

But for most of today she'd been on the edge and she knew it.

And now she felt as if something deep inside her had cracked open at his words, and all the pain, the anxiety and disappointment of the last weeks had come welling to the surface in one violent, cataclysmic surge that she was unable to repress.

A voice she didn't recognise as her own screamed, 'You utter bastard…' And she flung forward, launching herself wildly at him, hands curled into claws, striking at his face. Wanting to hurt him in return.

As she made contact, she heard him swear, then her wrists were seized in a punishing grip, and she was forced away from him, held at arm's length as the dark eyes raked her mercilessly.

His voice was harsh and breathless. 'You do not hit me—understand? You will never do so again, or I shall retaliate in a way you won't like.'

She tried to stare back defiantly, to twist free of his grasp, but his hold was relentless. And then she saw the smear of blood on his cheekbone and suddenly the enormity of what she'd done overwhelmed her.

She attempted to speak, but the only sound that escaped her was a choking sob, and the next instant she was crying in a way she'd never done before—loudly and gustily, all control abandoned, as the scalding tears stormed down her face.

He said icily, 'And now the usual woman's trick—weeping to get out of trouble. You disappoint me.'

He took her over to the sagging sofa at one side of the room, and pushed her down on to the elderly velvet cushions, tossing a handkerchief into her lap.

She was aware of him moving away, as another paroxysm shook her, and she buried her wet face in the soft square of linen. She could hear him moving about, followed by the chink of a bottle on glass, and then he was back, seating himself beside her, closing her fingers round a tumbler.

'Drink this.'

She tried to obey, but her hand was trembling too much.

He muttered something she did not understand, and raised the glass to her lips himself.

As the pungent smell reached her, Harriet recoiled. She said, her voice drowned and jerky, 'I don't drink spirits.'

'You do now.' He was inexorable.

She took one sip, and it was like swallowing liquid fire. She felt it burn all the way to her stomach, and flung her head back as he offered the glass again, saying hoarsely, 'No more—please.'

He put the glass down on the floor. 'So,' he said. 'This is more than just a drawing. What has happened to you?'

'Nothing that need concern you.' She scrubbed fiercely at her face with the handkerchief, trying to avoid looking at him directly. However, she was immediately aware that he was a little more dressed now than he had been before, in that he'd fastened the waistband of his jeans, pulled on another disreputable tee shirt, and had a pair of battered espadrilles on his feet.

But if this was a concession, it was a very minor one. It didn't make him appear any more civilised, or encourage her to feel any better about the situation. Or about him.

Oh, God, she thought with something like despair. What could have possessed her to do such an appalling thing? To have—flown at him like that, whatever the provocation. Then, worst of all, to have allowed herself to break down, and wail like a baby. How could she have behaved like that? It was as if she'd changed into a completely different person. And she wanted the old one back.

'But I am concerned.' He touched the mark on his cheek with a fingertip. 'See—I'm scarred already.'

'I'm—sorry,' she offered stiffly. And she was—but for letting herself down—not for hurting him. In fact, she wished she'd connected with her fist, instead of just a fingernail.

He gave her a sardonic look, as if he knew exactly what was going through her mind. 'A suggestion,' he said softly. 'Next time you're in scratching mood, my little tigress, make it my back, and not my face.'

As the implication in his words sank in, her face warmed with a blush she was powerless to prevent. Her fingers tightened, crushing the handkerchief into a damp ball. She needed to get out of there, she thought, before she embarrassed herself even further—if that were possible.

'I—I must be going.' She kept her voice artificially cool and clipped. 'I've a cab waiting for me.'

'I doubt that,' he said. 'But stay where you are, and I'll check if it's still there.'

She watched him go to the door with that lithe long-legged stride that she'd noticed in the restaurant. A realisation that disturbed her. And with his departure an odd stillness descended, as if the energy in the room had somehow gone with him.

He was, Harriet thought with a shiver, altogether too physical a presence. And it occurred to her that maybe she had got off lightly, after all.

On impulse, she pushed back the sleeves of her jacket, scanning her wrists and forearms for the marks of his fingers, but there were none, which surprised her. Although she could not speak, of course, for the emotional bruising she'd suffered.

But don't think about that, she told herself. Just concentrate on getting out of here.

She glanced around for her bag, and saw it lying where she'd dropped it, the contents spilling out across the floorboards, with the laptop case beside it. She crossed the room shakily, knelt and began to repack her bag. She'd check on the computer when she got home, but hopefully the outer padding would have saved it from serious damage.

As she rose, brushing off her skirt, she hesitated, taking another, closer look at her surroundings, and particularly at the paintings leaning against the walls that she'd seen on the periphery of her vision when she arrived.

And, as she soon realised with an odd excitement, they certainly repaid more thorough attention.

The majority of the paintings were abstracts, wild, ungovernable masses of colour applied to their canvases with an almost violent intensity, and, to Harriet, they were like experiencing an assault to the senses.

She went from one to another, aware that her arms were wrapped tightly round her body, as if she was warding off some danger. Knowing that, whether she liked them or not, they were impossible to ignore. She was being drawn to them unwillingly, she thought. Fascinated in spite of herself.

And there were landscapes too—bleak stretches of ochre-coloured earth, more bleached stones like the fallen columns of dead buildings, hard glittering sand bordering a dark and ominous sea. All battered by the light of that same brilliant and relentless sun that she'd seen in the original painting.

And that same sense of anger, barely contained, that she'd found emanating from him only a short while ago.

But this time no human element in any of the paintings. No trace that anyone had ever inhabited these alien environments.

They were raw—they were vital. But they belonged to no comfort zone that she knew. She could not imagine hanging one of them on the plain neutral walls of her determinedly minimalist flat. Or living with it afterwards, come to that.

She suddenly remembered a book she'd read as a child, where the young heroine stepped through the pictures in the gallery of an old house to find herself in the world they portrayed.

But to walk into the kind of barren burning wilderness that confronted her now would be a terrifying leap into the unknown—with the possibility that she might never be able to find her way back again. That she'd be trapped for all eternity in some living nightmare.

She shivered suddenly. My God, she thought in swift self-derision, am I letting my imagination run away with me here?

And it was no excuse to tell herself that it was sheer overreaction, because she'd been knocked sideways emotionally in all kinds of ways. Because the sheer power of these paintings could not be dismissed so easily.

He said, 'Your taxi's gone. But I called a local cab company. They are on their way.'

She whirled around as his voice reached her, her hand going to her mouth to stifle her startled cry. Because she'd had no idea he'd come back into the studio. Been far too absorbed to register his approach.

But he was there, leaning against the frame in the sunlit doorway, one hand negligently hooked in the waistband of his jeans, the other holding his mobile phone as he watched her.

Harriet snatched at what was left of her composure. She said stiltedly, 'Oh, right—thank you.' Then paused. 'I've been looking at your work. It's—good.' She recognised the lameness of that, and added hastily, 'In fact, it's probably far more than just good. It might be—amazing.'

'Does this signal that you are changing your opinion about me?' His mouth twisted mockingly. 'I'm flattered.'

'Well, don't be,' she returned curtly. 'I may recognise you have talent, but it doesn't follow that I have to like you any better.'

He winced elaborately. 'I see that the flood of tears was a temporary aberration. The real Miss Flint is back, and firing on all cylinders.'

'What I don't understand,' she went on, as if he hadn't spoken, 'is why you waste a moment of your time on those street portraits. They can't bring in enough money to pay the bills.'

'No,' he said. 'I look on them mainly as relaxation. It's good to get out sometimes—to meet new people. Don't you agree?'

She remembered the entranced face of the girl he'd been sketching outside the Flint Audley offices.

She looked round the big room, deliberately letting her glance linger on the pile of papers that had fallen off the sofa, the remains of a meal left on a table, the unmade bed, only half hidden behind a large folding screen. She said, 'And is this where you bring—your new friends?'

His tone was laconic as he followed her gaze. 'It's the maid's day off.'

'Then perhaps you should ask your girlfriend to clear up a little.' Her response was immediate—tart—and completely unintentional. After all, she'd already made her point.

'She does not come here for that,' he said gently. 'Also, she might spoil her beautiful hands, and I can put them to much better use.'

And no prizes for guessing what he meant, Harriet thought furiously, her face warming all over again in spite of herself. She said stonily, 'I always understood decent men did not kiss and tell.'

He shrugged, unrepentantly. 'Who mentioned kissing?' and laughed softly as her flush deepened.

He glanced over his shoulder as a car horn sounded from the street. 'And that is your cab, Miss Flint,' he added with studied politeness. 'Right on time.' And stood aside to let her pass.

Harriet found herself clinging to the rail of the metal staircase as she descended, aware that her legs were shaking, and that she was strangely breathless again.

As she crossed the yard, she looked back swiftly, almost furtively, to see if he was watching her go. But the staircase was empty, and the door was closed.

And for one confused, disturbing moment, Harriet did not know whether to be glad or sorry.

CHAPTER THREE

HIS handkerchief was a small, forlorn bundle in the middle of her gleaming ash table.

Harriet's instinct was to chuck it straight in the kitchen bin, possibly slamming down the lid as a coda, but she had to admit that current evidence suggested he might not have handkerchiefs to spare, and that it would be more gracious to return the damned thing laundered.

That was if she felt gracious.

And at the moment, in the seething maelstrom of her emotions, bewilderment seemed to predominate. Alongside anger.

She sank down into her black kid recliner chair, closing her eyes and allowing her whole body to go limp, while she breathed deeply and evenly, trying to recapture a modicum of calm and sanity.

She could not believe how her life had suddenly changed.

Twenty-four hours ago, she'd looked at the future with a kind of quiet confidence. She'd been about to take the next step up the ladder at Flint Audley, and she'd found a working solution to her grandfather's autocratic and ill-judged attempt to force her into matrimony.

Like the horse being led to water, she would get married. But not even Gregory Flint could force her to stay married, she'd told herself grimly. That was not part of the deal. Nor had he specified how long this unholy wedlock would have to last. But he could hardly insist she stayed in an unhappy relationship, especially if he believed his ultimatum was the root case of her misery.

Something she'd planned to make bravely and wistfully clear. How she'd been rushed into a terrible mistake.

Or that had been her intention, she thought bitterly.

Her precious, foolproof plan. Now wreckage.

The rung on the corporate ladder. Broken.

Oh, the expansion scheme would go ahead, but possibly not under her direction, however hard she worked on it. And maybe if there was a glass ceiling, Gramps had ordered its installation.

I wouldn't put it past him, she thought bleakly.

Perhaps she should have succumbed to the inevitable—picked one of the paralysingly dull but worthy young men who'd been regularly trotted out at dinner parties for her inspection. At least she'd have had the prospect of Gracemead as consolation.

But would that have been enough to reconcile her to the reality of marriage? Somehow she doubted it. She valued her independence too highly. Child as she'd been, she could remember only too well her mother's unavailing attempts to revive relationships that had clearly exceeded their shelf lives.

Maybe it was then that she'd realised the danger of being at the mercy of her hormones, she thought wryly.

And while life could be lonely at times, especially as most of her schoolfriends now seemed to have husbands and, accordingly, other priorities, at least she was at no one's beck and call when work was over. When her time became her own, along with her personal space.

And her time was now wasting.

She got up, and went into her bedroom, feeling her usual lift of satisfaction as she looked around her. All the furniture was built-in, and concealed behind anonymous doors, so the focal point was the bed. She'd picked the biggest she could find, with the most heavenly mattress, and dressed the whole thing in ivory linen, with olive green cushions adding the only colour note, one which she'd repeated in the shades of the lamps on the twin night tables flanking the bed.

The bathroom was equally austere in white and chrome, but she hadn't stinted on the size of the tub, or the walk-in shower, and particularly on the pile of fluffy towels that were always waiting.

She undressed slowly, dropping her clothes into the linen basket, loosened her hair from its constricting band, and stepped under the fierce pelting of the shower, first smothering herself in her favourite scented body wash. How wonderful, she thought, as she turned herself languorously under the warm torrent, if the troubles of the day could be as easily rinsed away as this foam.

She dried herself, and put on a pair of her favourite pyjamas. She had a whole range of them, tailored in satin in cool pastel shades, and obtained from an exclusive mail order source, and tonight's choice was pale turquoise.

She padded barefoot into her gleaming kitchen, taking a ready-cooked chicken breast from the fridge, preparing a dressing for the accompanying salad, and heating a small baguette. If she wanted dessert, there was always yoghurt.

As she ate, she pondered what she could put in tomorrow's report for Tony. Nothing, for sure, that would sound like an excuse, or make it sound as if she wasn't up to the job. She'd believed until today that they had a good working relationship based on mutual respect. Now it seemed as if he'd just been waiting for her to screw up.

Well, she was not so easily to be set aside, she told herself defiantly. She would fight, and fight again, and to hell with glass ceilings.

Because iron had entered her soul that afternoon, when she'd discovered what people really thought about her, and now she no longer merely wanted to take charge of the expansion plans. No, she wouldn't be content now until she held the position her grandfather had once enjoyed—as chairman of the board.

At which point, they'd be laughing on the other side of their faces.

Her meal ended, she put on some Mozart and set to work, drafting and re-drafting the report for Tony until she was reasonably satisfied. She kept it short and pithy, maintaining the basic value of the scheme, but admitting she'd failed to gauge the level of opposition it might garner. That she felt this had been based on personalities rather than actual reasoning, and that next time she would ensure that opinion was more informed, so that there could be a genuine debate.

Then she printed it off, closed down her laptop, and sat back with a sigh, closing her eyes.

One rock shifted, hopefully, but a massive boulder still to go.

Keeping her job might be one thing. But hanging on to Gracemead was quite another, especially when her grandfather's deadline was coming nearer by the day.

She supposed she could always try another small ad on one of the dating pages, then recalled with a grimace just how long it had taken to extract Peter from among the welter of total unsuitables who'd responded. None of whom she'd wish to encounter a second time.

Also, she had to be careful. If, by some remote but fatal chance, anyone at work found out or even suspected what she was trying to do, her life would become completely unbearable. And outside work she never met any men. Apart, of course, from today…

She sat up with a jolt, as if several hundred volts of electricity had suddenly passed through her, her mind going into overdrive.

Then stopped, as she remembered contemptuous dark eyes. A voice that dripped scorn. And took a deep breath. No, she thought, that's nonsensical. That's carrying the whole thing to the limits of absurdity. Don't even consider it.

But the idea refused to go away. It nagged at her for the remainder of the evening, and even followed her to bed, where she lay, staring sleeplessly into the darkness as she continued to argue with herself.

On the face of it, she and this Roan had nothing in common, except their mutual antipathy. But he needed a boost to his career as an artist, which she might—just—be able to supply. And he was a good painter. He had a real gift. Whatever her personal opinion of him as a man, she was certain of that at least.

And if she was prepared to help him, she was surely entitled to ask for his assistance in return, even though she could guess his probable reaction when he learned the details, she thought, wincing.

But she'd simply have to stress that their dislike of each other was a positive advantage under the circumstances. And that any acceptance of her terms would be strictly business.

After all, she told herself grimly, she didn't want that appalling male arrogance, which seemed as natural to him as breathing, to persuade him for one second that she found him even remotely attractive.

His pretty blonde might be a snag, of course, but she could hardly raise any real objections to the scheme, as she was married herself.

And as she turned over, punching the pillow into submission, a name came floating into her mind, reminding her of someone in the art world she might approach. 'Desmond Slevin,' she murmured with drowsy satisfaction, and closed her eyes, smiling.

The following morning brought a few misgivings, but no real second thoughts.

If he chose to co-operate, this Roan could secure Gracemead for her after all. Therefore she had to pursue the idea that had come to her last night.

At the office, having meekly handed her report to Tony, and attended to any urgent business, she did a quick computer check on her designated prey.

Desmond Slevin, an art dealer and collector, who owned the Parsifal Gallery in the West End, was a former tenant now living in Surrey.

Harriet had read a piece about him quite recently in one of the broadsheets, describing him as one of the treasure seekers of the art world, always on the look-out for new and gifted painters. If it was true, he might be just the man she needed.

Accordingly, she took an early lunch, and grabbed a passing taxi to whisk her to the gallery. And a few minutes later she was sitting in Desmond Slevin's private office, drinking coffee.

'So, what can I do for you, Miss Flint?' He was a handsome middle-aged man on the verge of being elderly, with grey hair, and piercing blue eyes. 'Are you here to persuade me to give up the commute and rent another London pad?'

Harriet returned his smile. 'I doubt that I could. No, I read a recent article about you, and it—got me thinking.'

'Oh.' He pulled a face. 'Frankly, I came to regret that interview.' He gave her a narrow-eyed glance. 'I trust you haven't taken up painting as a hobby, because you were once very kind and helpful, and I'd hate to disappoint you.'

She laughed. 'You're quite safe, I promise.' And paused. 'But if I ever saw work that seemed to have real talent, might you be interested in—perhaps—taking a look?'

He said dryly, 'And I'm wondering, in turn, if that question is quite as hypothetical as it sounds.' He refilled her cup. 'So, who is this undiscovered genius, Miss Flint? A boyfriend?'

'God, no.' Harriet sat bolt upright, nearly spilling her coffee down her skirt. Bright spots of colour burned in her face. 'The exact opposite, in fact. Someone I barely know. I—I don't even have his full name.'

'Dear me,' he said placidly. 'All the same he seems to have made quite an impression.' He watched her reflectively for a moment. 'Is there a body of work involved?'

'Yes, I suppose—I think so. He—he has a studio.'

He laughed. 'Which doesn't always mean much. Does he know that you've come to see me on his behalf?'

'No,' she admitted. 'It was just an impulse, really.'

'So you don't know whether he'd be interested in selling his work?'

'Well, of course he would. Why ever not?'

Desmond Slevin's sigh held a touch of cynicism. 'My dear, I've met many in my time who feel their work is unique, and of far too lofty significance to be handled commercially. Therefore I find it's always best to check in advance.'

'I don't think that would apply in this case.' Harriet drew a deep breath. 'So, if I talk to him first, would you be willing to see his paintings? Give an opinion?'

'Yes,' he said slowly. 'Why not?' He raised a minatory finger. 'Just as long as you both understand that it doesn't necessarily mean a deal.'

'Oh, I'll make that very clear.'

'Then I'll wait to hear from you,' he said, and rose.

'You know,' he said as he accompanied her through the gallery to the street door. 'It occurs to me you're going to a lot of trouble for a complete stranger.' He paused, and patted her on the shoulder. 'But I'm sure you know your own business best.'

I wouldn't count on it, Harriet thought grimly as she pinned on a beaming smile and walked away. In fact, I might well be making one of life's more serious mistakes.

If, in fact, she went through with it. Because, as she kept reminding herself, she didn't have to do this. She could still pull out, and no harm done. Tell Desmond Slevin that, after all, the paintings hadn't repaid a second, closer inspection, and she was sorry for wasting his time. A smile and a shrug, and it would be all over.

But so would Gracemead, as a telephone conversation with her grandfather that same evening swiftly confirmed. Because if she'd hoped that his attitude might be softening at this late stage, she was gravely disappointed. He was still completely adamant in his views.

'Stay a career woman if that's what you want, Harriet,' he told her brusquely. 'Although I hear even that isn't going so well these days. Live alone in that bleak flat of yours. But you'll have no need of a family house and Gracemead can be put to better use.'

She put the phone down feeling sick at heart, and not just about the house. His comment about her work had struck a chill too.

So, gritting her teeth, she sat down to bait her hook. But what could she say to tempt him? I have a proposal for you? No, too blatant. A proposition? God, even worse.

And where could they meet? She didn't want to go to his studio again. Somewhere public would be preferable. Even essential. A restaurant maybe? But for lunch, perhaps, rather than dinner. Or was that all too social?

Eventually she came up with a form of words which would have to do. And she was annoyed to find her hand shaking as she dialled his mobile number. It was almost a relief to find she was speaking to his voicemail.

She said steadily, 'This is Harriet Flint. I have a business matter I would like to discuss with you, which could be to your advantage. Perhaps you would meet me for afternoon tea on Saturday at the Titan Palace Hotel, at four-thirty.' She hesitated, then added, 'If this is inconvenient, please contact me at Flint Audley between nine and six to arrange another appointment.'

Well, that was brisk and businesslike enough, which was why

she'd chosen the Titan Palace as an appropriate rendezvous. As one of the capital's newest hotels, it was large, impersonal and catering for an upmarket business clientele. A place where deals were done.

Also, afternoon tea sounded very correct and English. Fairly aloof, too, so he couldn't possibly infer that he was being asked out on some kind of date.

Although there was still no guarantee, of course, that he'd turn up, no matter how she phrased the invitation.

But Saturday arrived with no cancellation, so it seemed they were destined for another confrontation after all.

Harriet went through the predominantly black contents of her wardrobe several times before deciding on a pair of taupe linen trousers, with a matching thigh-length jacket worn over a stone coloured tee shirt. Neutral but neat.

Besides, one odious comparison with a bat was quite sufficient in anybody's lifetime, she thought, her mouth tightening.

For a moment, she contemplated leaving her hair loose, then decided it was probably wiser to wear it in her usual style, severely drawn back from her face. And definitely no cosmetics.

She got to the appointment early, and took a seat in the hotel's vast lounge, where she could keep a beady eye on the main entrance into the hotel foyer.

It was an impressive place, she thought, glancing round her, and busy too. Afternoon teas were clearly doing a roaring trade, and the soft sounds of a pianist playing gentle jazz were only just audible above the hum of conversation. But a crowd she could blend into was exactly what she wanted.

Although it was never her intention to become invisible, she thought with faint irritation, as she made another of several vain attempts to catch the eye of a scurrying waiter.

And as she settled back into her chair with a sigh, she suddenly realised that Roan was there, walking towards her. Was aware too of an odd stillness at his approach, with people leaning towards each other at neighbouring tables, and murmuring.

But maybe they were simply planning to have him thrown out for breaking some dress code, she thought with disfavour. The jeans he was wearing were elderly, but clean, fitting him like a second skin, and his white shirt had at least one too many buttons undone. The cuffs were casually turned back, revealing bronzed forearms, and his bare feet were thrust into espadrilles. He still needed a haircut, and a shave wouldn't have gone amiss either. Yet for all that…

Barring any such thought, she got hurriedly to her feet. 'Hi.' She tried to sound nonchalant. 'So you came after all.'

The dark eyes glinted at her. 'Wasn't that the idea?'

'Yes, of course. Please sit down.' She sounded as if she was conducting a job interview, but maybe that was the correct note to use, she thought as she resumed her own seat. 'I've been trying to order tea, but—'

She broke off as he lifted a languid hand, and two waiters came running, as if all they'd been waiting for was his signal.

'The lady would like tea. Coffee for me, please.'

Harriet, bewildered and pardonably annoyed, watched the deference with which his instructions were received.

'How did you manage that?' she asked.

'It wasn't difficult.' He leaned back in his chair. 'Do you wish to begin our discussion now, or shall we talk about the weather until we have been served?'

'Now would be best, perhaps,' she said stiffly. 'You must be wondering why I asked for this meeting.'

His brows lifted sardonically. 'I am breathless with curiosity.'

Harriet bit her lip—hard, then addressed herself to the prepared script. 'First of all,' she said, 'I need to apologise for my behaviour at our last meeting. I can only say that I've been under a great deal of pressure lately, and your sketch of me was…'

'The last straw?' he supplied helpfully as she hesitated.

'Well, yes,' she agreed. *Although unforgivable was what I really had in mind.* 'I want you to know that I don't usually lose my temper in such a way.'

'Reassuring,' he said. 'But did you bring me all the way across London just to tell me that?'

'No, of course not.' She swallowed. 'I really want to talk about your work. You see, I wasn't pretending when I said it was good, and I—I've mentioned it to an acquaintance of mine, who owns quite a well-known gallery—the Parsifal. You may have heard of it.'

'Yes.' The monosyllable gave nothing away.

Harriet ploughed on. 'Anyway there's a chance—if he also thinks you're good—that he might stage an exhibition for you. Get you launched.'

At which point, the waiters returned. Plates of tiny finger sandwiches, scones, and cakes oozing cream were placed on the table, along with tea for Harriet, and a pot of coffee served black for her companion.

When they were finally alone again, she said, 'You do realise what could be on offer here. Haven't you—anything to say?'

'I think I'm stunned,' he returned slowly. 'Also wary.'

'It's all perfectly genuine,' she protested. 'He's a prominent figure in the art world. If he decides to feature you at his gallery, it would be a terrific break for your career.'

'Undoubtedly,' he said. 'But what I need to know is why you, of all people, should have recommended me to this person. I find it puzzling.'

'I feel you have talent which should be recognised. I'd like to play my part in that—recognition.'

She didn't sound particularly convincing, she thought, vexed, but then the conversation was not going exactly as planned either. How can I ever thank you? was actually the response she'd been hoping for, if not depending on.

'Ah,' he said softly. 'Is it really that simple?' He shook his head. 'Somehow I doubt it. Because I have to tell you, Miss Flint, that you are not my idea of a philanthropist.'

She sat very still. She said, 'Then you're not interested in this offer?'

'Interested, yes, but not overwhelmed. You must understand I need to find out what you expect in return.' His smile seemed to skin her to the bone. 'In case the price is more than I'm prepared to pay.'

So that was that. For a moment she felt completely numb, then she reached for her bag. 'In that case, there's nothing more to be said. I'm sorry I've wasted your time.'

'Now you're being a fool,' he drawled. 'If you want me to

consider your terms, I suggest you stay where you are. Do what the British generally do at a crisis, and drink some tea.'

For a moment, she was tempted to storm out, having first emptied the teapot over his head, then she remembered what was at stake here and reluctantly subsided, giving him a muted glare.

'Has anyone told you that you're insolent?' she enquired coldly.

He shrugged. 'And you, Miss Flint, are clearly both devious and determined,' he retorted. 'Let us accept that neither of us is perfect, and move on.'

She took a breath. 'I have—a problem. I need a husband.'

He stared at her, eyes narrowed. 'Then the answer is simple. Get married.'

'But I don't want to be married, not now, not ever.' She spoke with quiet vehemence. 'However, I don't have a choice.' She paused. 'So, I need someone prepared to go through a marriage ceremony with me, then get out of my life.'

'And I clearly need more coffee,' he said. 'Or even something stronger. Unless, of course, you can promise me that you have not, even for a moment, cast me in this unlikely role.'

'Listen to me—please.' She leaned forward. 'It's a form of words in a register office—that's all. We say them—and we split. When the marriage has served its purpose, we divorce. And I pay all the expenses.

'What's more, I'll pay you an additional lump sum big enough for you to stage your own exhibition, if the Parsifal Gallery isn't interested in your work, or to spend in any other way you please. That's not a variable. You really won't lose out over this.'

There was a silence, then he said, 'Tell me, Miss Flint, how long did it take for you to invent this incredible fantasy?'

She shook her head. 'No fantasy. I'm deadly serious. And desperate.'

'I was afraid of that,' he said grimly. 'But why?' His dark gaze seemed to drill into hers. 'And please do not say it does not concern me, when it clearly does.'

Harriet pushed away her untouched tea. 'Very well—if you must know,' she acceded reluctantly, 'unless I'm married by my twenty-fifth birthday, I stand to lose something that means the world to me.'

She swallowed. 'My grandfather, who operates from the Dark Ages, insists that he will not allow me to inherit my childhood home if I don't have a husband to help with the running of the estate. He feels a family house would be wasted on a single woman, and that I might fall prey to unscrupulous—people.'

'You think a husband picked off the streets would not fall into this category?'

'Naturally, I would insist on a strict pre-nuptial agreement.'

'Oh, naturally,' he said. His expression was deadpan but there was a slight tremor in his voice.

She gave him a suspicious glare. 'You seem to think it's funny.'

'No,' he said. 'I think it's tragic.' He paused. 'And your birthday is—when?'

'In six weeks' time.'

'Strange,' he said. 'I would have thought you much younger.' He added coolly, 'And that is not intended as a compliment.'

'Fortunately, your opinion of me doesn't matter. My only concern is Gracemead.' She looked down at her clasped hands. 'I actually found someone to marry through a personal ad, but a few days ago he suddenly backed out—and now I'm stranded.'

'Or had a lucky escape,' he suggested unsmilingly.

'I saw it as a no-risk strategy,' Harriet said defiantly. 'Where we both gain. I still do.'

He said harshly. 'Then I am not surprised your grandfather wishes you to have a husband. I am only astonished he allows you to go about without a keeper.'

'How—how dare you?' Her voice shook. 'If that's all you can say, let's forget the whole thing.'

'Not so fast,' he said, and there was a note in his voice that stopped her unwillingly in her tracks. 'I presume that my introduction to this gallery owner depends on my acquiescence to this monstrous plan—am I right?'

'Naturally,' she returned curtly. 'That's the deal on the table. A straightforward *quid pro quo*.'

'I do not think we share the same understanding of "straightforward",' he drawled. 'How much are you planning to pay in cash for my compliance? I ask only because I have never been for sale before, and I wish to savour the experience—to the full.'

She sat up very straight. 'The exact terms have to be agreed, but I think you'll find me generous,' she said.

'Yes,' he said softly. 'I am quite sure that I will.'

She found his faint smile distinctly unnerving, and continued hastily, 'Afterwards we would live and work exactly as we do now— apart.' She coloured a little. 'And of course you'd be free to conduct your—private life just as you wish. I wouldn't dream of imposing any restrictions on your personal conduct.'

'You are too gracious, Miss Flint.' His voice was soft, but there was an edge to it. 'And I would also be expected to turn a blind eye if you chose to take a lover? Is that what you're saying?'

She frowned. 'Well, no. I mean—how could you possibly know? It's not as if we'll be meeting at any point before we divorce.' She added with constraint, 'And, anyway, it won't happen. I have no intention of becoming involved in that kind of relationship.'

'So sex has no place in your life,' he murmured, his lips twisting. 'Well that, perhaps, explains your unpleasant temper.'

She said icily, 'And that, if I may say so, is a typically male viewpoint.'

'But I am a man, Miss Flint. What else do you expect?' He paused. 'Let us return to essentials. Do you truly believe your grandfather will quietly accept the appearance in your life of some complete stranger? That he will not smell a very large and very pungent rat?'

She shrugged defensively. 'He's put his demands in writing. They say nothing about the nature of the relationship, just that it should legally exist. Nor does he mention the length of time any marriage should last. And that's where he made his mistake.'

She lifted her chin. 'He thinks he has me over a barrel, but he has to learn that I'm my own woman, and he can't control me in this way. Also that no contract is entirely foolproof.'

'Then for once we are in agreement.' His tone was ironic. 'But we might differ on who may turn out to be the fool in all this.'

He was silent for a long moment, tapping his fingers restlessly on the table, his glance flickering thoughtfully over her.

At last, 'Very well, Miss Flint,' he said quietly. 'Crazy as it is, I accept your proposal. I will marry you on the terms discussed.'

'Thank you,' she said. 'I am—more than grateful.'

Hs glance was frankly cynical. 'I think that remains to be seen.' He paused. 'As we are now officially engaged, am I permitted to call you Harriet?'

'Yes,' she said. 'Of course.' She flushed. 'And I need to know the rest of your name—for when I break the good news to my grandfather.'

'I am Zandros,' he said. 'Roan Zandros.' He leaned forward, offering his hand, and before she realised what she was doing Harriet allowed her fingers to be clasped by his. His touch was warm and strong, and in spite of herself she felt her pulses leap in an unexpected and unwelcome response.

And saw his firm mouth slant, as if he'd gauged her reaction, and was amused by it.

He said softly, 'To our better acquaintance, Harriet *mou*.' Then, before she could free herself, he raised her hand almost ceremoniously to his lips and kissed it, leaving her gasping.

CHAPTER FOUR

'WHAT on earth are you doing?' Harriet snatched back her hand, furiously aware that she was blushing.

'A formal seal to our betrothal.' He sounded completely unconcerned. 'That is all.'

'Thank you,' she said grittily. 'Perhaps we can dispense with any further formalities.'

He was grinning now. 'Of course, if that is what you wish.'

'Yes,' she said. 'It is.' Something told her she was being absurd to make such a fuss over so little. After all, the kiss had barely lasted a second. Yet she had a curious conviction that if she looked at her hand she would see the mark of his mouth burning like a brand on her skin.

Anxious to dismiss the incident, she hurried into speech. 'Zandros—that's a Greek name?'

'You seem surprised.'

'No, not really,' she said quickly. 'It's just that—you speak English so well.'

'I had an English mother, and I spent a lot of time in this country when I was young. Also, it was where I began my education.'

'Oh,' she said. 'I see.'

'I don't think so,' Roan said, not unkindly. 'But there is no reason why you should.' He paused. 'So, when do you plan to tell your grandfather about this sudden change in your circumstances?'

'I'll go down next weekend and talk to him.'

He nodded meditatively. 'And how will you explain me? I cannot be the grandson he had in mind.'

'No,' Harriet agreed. 'Quite the contrary, which makes it all the better.'

His glance held faint reproof. 'In your view, perhaps. But if I may offer some advice,' he added dryly, 'you should not gloat too openly over your victory. A man does not like to find himself bested by a woman.'

'Too bad,' she said. 'But it's hardly that, because I'm doing exactly what he wants. So how can he complain if I interpret that in my own way?'

'Experience suggests he may complain very bitterly. Does your desire for this pile of bricks and mortar really justify causing such upset?'

Harriet looked down at the table. She said constrictedly, 'Don't get me wrong. I love him—I really do. But he doesn't understand my need to live as an independent woman, and he never has. He has to accept that.'

'And your parents? What have they to say about this?'

She said, 'They're—no longer around.'

He glanced at her frowningly. 'I am sorry.'

'Don't be,' she said brightly. 'I've had years to grow accustomed to it.'

'You are fortunate. My mother died nearly three years ago, and she is still constantly in my thoughts.' He leaned back in his chair, his gaze watchful. 'This house you want so much—without marriage, who will be there to inherit it when you are gone?'

She said defensively, 'I could always adopt a child.'

'A single woman?' His brows rose. 'Does the law allow this?'

'Why not? After all, I shan't be poor, and money opens all kinds of doors.'

'Yes,' he said. 'I am beginning to see that.' His smile was ironic. 'But, as one of those doors has opened for me, I can hardly complain.' He paused again. 'You do not think that one day you will meet a man you can love, and wish to have his babies?'

'No,' Harriet said shortly. 'I don't. And may we please leave my personal foibles to one side, and get back to business? I'd already started on the arrangements when I thought I was going to marry—the other man, but there's still a great deal to do.' She looked down at her bare hands. 'For one thing, I need a ring.'

'That is usually the bridegroom's responsibility,' he said. 'Therefore, you may leave it to me.'

'It's hardly an expense you can afford,' she returned. 'Besides, you don't know the correct size.'

'I could make an educated guess.' He looked her over, eyes narrowed. 'As I could do about the size of everything you are wearing at this moment. Do you wish me to demonstrate?'

She was infuriated to realise that her face was burning again. She said with a snap, 'No, thank you.' She got to her feet, and he stood up too, making her aware all over again of how tall he was, and how broad his shoulders were under the cling of his shirt. She added hurriedly, 'There'll be things to sign—papers and such. My lawyer will contact you.'

She paused. 'The date of the wedding—is there any particular day of the week that you'd find inconvenient?'

'You are most considerate,' he said courteously. 'However, I will make quite sure I'm available when you require me to be so.'

'Then I'll arrange for Mr Slevin to come to your studio,' she said. 'I—I hope the visit goes well. His backing would be such a fantastic boost for you.'

She realised she was babbling again, and stopped, rummaging inside her bag for her wallet instead. She put some notes on the table. 'That should cover the bill.' She sent him a bright, meaningless smile. 'If you want to order anything else, please do so.'

For an instant, there was an odd silence—almost a tension in the air. Then Roan bent his head in polite acknowledgement, and the moment passed.

All the same, her goodbye was faintly uncertain as she took her departure. And as she emerged into the street, she found she was strangely breathless.

But why? she wondered. Because I should be cheering, now that I've solved my problem at last.

Except, she reminded herself as she signalled to a passing taxi, that I still have to tell Grandfather.

The week that followed was a busy one. Harriet spent the latter part of it in the Midlands, revisiting the sites she'd targeted on earlier trips, and taking extensive photographs to accompany her redrafted report, when it was prepared, and support its recommendations. Nothing this time would be left to chance, she thought with grim determination. Whatever the questions, she would have all the answers.

However, in spite of this resolution, she seemed to be finding concentration difficult, particularly as she wasn't sleeping too well at nights.

Clearly the forthcoming confrontation with her grandfather must be preying on her mind rather more than she'd expected, she told herself wryly.

When she got back to London on Friday afternoon, the atmosphere at Flint Audley was festive. Gina, who worked in Accounting, was having a birthday, and a cake, complete with candles, had been cut up and passed around the office at teatime. And after work, everyone was going out for a celebratory drink. Or all except one…

'We didn't think you'd be back,' Gina informed Harriet off-handedly. 'But you're welcome to join us—if you want,' she added, eying Harriet's serviceable black pants and tunic top with ill-concealed disfavour.

'Thank you,' Harriet returned with equal insincerity. 'But I'm going down to the country this evening.'

'Off to the stately pile?' Jon Audley joined them, his smile malicious. 'Dad always thought it would divide up into great flats, and I'm sure he was right. There's even enough land to construct a nine-hole golf course as a total bonus. Something to bear in mind when it finally falls into your waiting hands, Harriet dear.'

She looked back at him evenly. 'Except that Gracemead is not for sale,' she said. 'Not now. Not ever.'

'Always supposing you have the choice,' he murmured, and walked away, leaving her staring after him, more shaken than she cared to admit. Had rumours of her grandfather's intentions some-how reached Flint Audley?

If so, it would give her intense pleasure to prove them unfounded.

Because, whether Gregory Flint liked it or not, he would have to accept her unlikely bridegroom.

Her own attitude to him, however, seemed less easy to define.

While she'd been away, she'd found Roan Zandros in her thoughts far more than she wished. She wasn't altogether sure she hadn't dreamed about him, but, if so, her memories were thankfully hazy.

She could only be certain that he wasn't what she'd had in mind when she originally devised her plan.

And in some ways she wished he'd turned her down, and walked away.

Oh, come on, she adjured herself impatiently. That's defeatist thinking. He's a means to an end, that's all. A business deal. And you'll have a firewall to protect you anyway, with your pre-nuptial agreement.

Back at the flat, she showered quickly and shampooed her hair. She'd intended to wear it up, or braid it, but she was running late, so she decided for once simply to brush it and leave it loose.

There was a beige linen shift dress in her wardrobe, and she changed into it with reluctance, her grandfather's preferences and prejudices at the forefront of her mind. He preferred her to wear skirts, and there was no point in getting off on the wrong foot, and upsetting him over something as trivial as her choice of clothing.

However, he'd sounded genuinely pleased when she phoned to say she was coming down. Their recent meetings had been less frequent than usual, and overshadowed by the inevitable tensions arising from his ultimatum.

Maybe he hoped that some kind of reconciliation was on the cards, and, if so, she would listen. But only if he relented sufficiently to let her off the hook.

She bit her lip. It was far more likely that she'd have to proceed with her bargain, and go through a wedding ceremony with Roan Zandros.

After which, her life would just—continue as usual.

While she packed her weekend case, she listened to the messages on her answering machine. An investment group was offering her a financial health check. Her oldest friend Tessa wanted her to come to dinner. 'Bill says it's been far too long, and he's right, Harry, love. Where does the time go, I ask myself? So call us.'

And her lawyer, Isobel Crane, had also phoned, to tell her that the pre-nuptial agreement had been prepared according to her instructions, and was ready for signature, but might need further discussion.

In other words, she wants to talk me out of the whole thing, Harriet thought, her lips twisting wryly. Well, nothing new there.

She was a little disappointed that there was no message from Desmond Slevin, who'd been planning to visit Roan's studio two days earlier. But he was a busy man, she told herself, and maybe there'd been no opportunity as yet. It was certainly too soon to give up hope.

Besides, whatever Desmond's decision, Roan Zandros would get his exhibition. That was the deal, and whatever it cost, it would be worth it.

At least, that's what I have to believe, she thought, and realised with shock that it was the first time she'd even been remotely doubtful about what she was doing.

And her doubts multiplied on the way down, so that when she drove into the village a couple of hours later, she felt almost sick with nerves. Any sense of triumph had long since dissipated. Now she was simply doing what she must to safeguard her inheritance.

When she reached Gracemead, she parked at the rear of the house, near the old stable block, and went in through the kitchen to be met by the enticing aroma of roast duck, unless she missed her guess.

Mrs Wade, a little stouter and greyer, was whipping thick cream to accompany the chocolate mousse which was one of her masterpieces. She greeted Harriet with affection, and told her that Mr Flint was in the drawing room.

'With his visitor, Miss Harriet,' she added.

Harriet grimaced inwardly. She'd hoped to have her grandfather all to herself, so she could break the news about her wedding before she lost her nerve. But maybe his company wouldn't stay long.

She dropped her case in the hall, and went into the drawing room, only to find it empty. But the French windows were standing open to the evening sun, and she could hear the faint rumble of her grandfather's voice coming from the terrace outside.

Taking a deep breath, she went out to join him.

Gregory Flint was standing at the balustrade, gesturing expansively as he indicated points of interest in the gardens spread out before them to the man at his side, too wrapped up in one of his favourite topics to notice her arrival.

Although she could only see his companion's back, she knew instinctively that he was not one of the locals, but someone she'd never seen before, tall and soberly suited, a dark silhouette against the sunset's brightness.

A complete stranger, she thought. Or was he…?

She halted suddenly, staring at the strong shoulders and narrow hips set off by some expensive tailoring. Feeling her mouth turn dry as her brain tried to reject the evidence being presented by her eyes. Telling herself—no—it wasn't—couldn't be possible…

And as if aware of her scrutiny, he turned slowly and looked at her as she stood, hesitating, by the drawing room windows.

'Agapi mou,' Roan Zandros said, smiling, and walked towards her, his dark eyes sweeping over her in a frank appraisal that reminded her that it was the first time he'd seen her wearing a dress, and also that her hair had dried into a waving, unruly cloud on her shoulders. The lingering look he was bestowing on her legs as he approached only served to add outrage to her anger at this unwarranted intrusion—here at her home, her sanctuary.

She managed the single word, 'What—?' before his arms went round her, pulling her towards him, and jerking the breath out of her.

He bent towards her, shielding her with his body to give the impression that they were locked in a passionate embrace, as he stared down into her frantically widening eyes. His mouth an indrawn breath from hers, he whispered, 'Smile, Harriet. Pretend you are pleased to see me.'

Then he swung her round, his arm holding her firmly, his hand resting on her hip in a gesture of unmistakable possession, as they faced her grandfather together.

'Well, my dear.' Gregory Flint's tone might be mild, but his eyes were watchful under their shaggy brows. 'I gather from this young man that I must wish you happiness.' He paused. 'I confess I had no idea that there was anyone in your life, and this visit came as a complete surprise to me.'

And to me, thought Harriet as she lifted her chin, her gaze meeting his with a serenity she was far from feeling. 'A pleasant one, I hope, Grandfather.'

'I hope so too,' he agreed dryly. 'I told your fiancé frankly, Harriet, that he was not what I had expected, but he assures me that his prospects are excellent, and I am obliged to believe him.'

Roan said quietly, 'Harriet has been away, and therefore does not know that Desmond Slevin has agreed to exhibit my work at the Parsifal Gallery. I heard from him today.'

'Oh.' Harriet swallowed. 'Well, that's wonderful news. I'm— delighted for you. Darling,' she added belatedly.

Roan's smile did not reach his eyes. 'And I owe all my good fortune to you, my sweet one.' He turned back to Gregory Flint. 'I hope, sir, we have your consent to our marriage—and your blessing.'

'For what it's worth—yes.' There was a hint of grimness in Gregory Flint's faint smile. 'I'm sure any opinion of mine will make no difference at all to your plans.'

He looked at his watch. 'Dinner will be in forty minutes. Why don't you show Mr Zandros the garden, my dear, and enjoy your reunion in private? I expect you have a lot to talk about.'

Roan held her arm as they descended the shallow stone steps leading to the lawn. He said very softly, 'If you wish to attack me, Harriet *mou*, I suggest you wait. And don't pull away from me. We are still under surveillance.'

'How dare you?' she muttered furiously in return, her entire body rigid. 'How dare you—barge in like this?'

'No barging was necessary,' he returned calmly. 'I rang the bell, and was admitted like any other visitor.'

'But how did you find your way here in the first place?'

'It wasn't difficult. I knew your grandfather's name, and that of the house. I simply—made enquiries.'

'I think you must have gone completely mad.' She shook her

head. 'Whatever possessed you to come here—and ask his permission, for God's sake? I feel as if I'm taking part in some costume drama on television.'

'From what you have told me,' he said slowly, 'it seemed that your grandfather was an old-fashioned man, who might prefer such a gesture instead of merely being told of your decision—which he might interpret as deliberate provocation.'

'Oh, you know so much about it, naturally.' She tugged herself free, no longer caring if they were being watched.

He shrugged a shoulder. 'I've dealt with autocrats before. Pitched battles are rarely the answer.' He smiled at her. 'An element of surprise is often more successful.'

Yes, she thought, seething. I've just discovered that for myself.

Aloud, she said, 'It didn't occur to you to consult me first?'

'You were not around to consult, Harriet *mou*,' he pointed out, his tone infuriatingly reasonable. 'Besides, I was certain you would refuse.'

'How right you were,' she said stormily, and relapsed into another simmering silence. At the same time, she took her first proper look at him.

Little wonder she hadn't recognised him immediately, she thought in bewilderment. Because there wasn't a scrap of torn denim or a paint stain in sight. The charcoal suit he was wearing might not be new, but it was unmistakably elegant. His white shirt was crisp, his tie was silk, and his shoes, amazingly, were polished. He even appeared—dear God—to be wearing socks.

His hair was still too long, at least by Gregory Flint's exacting standards, but it had been trimmed, and he was immaculately shaven. During those few unpleasant seconds when she'd been in his arms, she'd been aware of a faint, beguiling hint of expensive cologne.

In fact she had to admit that he scrubbed up quite well, she thought reluctantly, then realised that he was watching her in turn, his smile widening as if he'd guessed exactly what she was thinking.

Embarrassment prompted her into waspishness. 'So where did you get the clothes—some upmarket charity shop?'

'I thought you would be pleased,' he said, 'to find me correctly dressed for my part. As you are too, Harriet *mou*,' he added dryly. 'For once you have decided to abandon your usual camouflage and look like a woman.'

She managed to turn her instinctive gasp into a deep breath. She said stonily, 'May I remind you that we have a strictly business arrangement, and therefore sexist remarks are neither required nor appreciated?'

His tone was silky. 'But sometimes irresistible, nonetheless. And now shall we continue to explore the grounds? They are very beautiful.'

'Is that what it's all about—this unexpected visit?' She swung to face him again. 'To assess the estate, and see what extra pickings there might be? Because, if so, you'll be disappointed, Mr Zandros. You get your exhibition and some money in your pocket, but nothing more. The pre-nuptial agreement I've had drawn up gives you no other claim.'

He remained annoyingly unfazed. 'I cannot wait to read this fascinating document,' he said softly. 'However, I came here solely out of curiosity, Harriet *mou*. I wished to see for myself what there could be about this place that would make you to risk so much for its possession.' He gestured around him. 'Can this really be all that constitutes happiness for you?'

'I don't expect you to understand,' she said defiantly. 'Besides, it's none of your business.'

'I think you made it my business when you asked me to marry you.'

'Well, we're not likely to agree about that,' Harriet said coldly. 'As a matter of interest, just how long are you planning to stay?'

'I leave in the morning. I have work to do for the exhibition.' He paused. 'Does that reassure you?'

'Not particularly,' she said. 'So, let me make something clear. This will be your first and last visit to this house. When you go tomorrow, you do not come back—on any pretext.'

'I think that is a decision for your grandfather to make,' Roan said with equal iciness. 'You do not rule here yet, Harriet *mou*. Maybe you should remember that.' He paused, his dark gaze sweeping over her with something like contempt in its depths. 'And now I find I would prefer to continue my tour of this garden alone. Your company does nothing for the beauty of the landscape.'

And he walked away, leaving her staring after him, open-mouthed, as she searched for a riposte that would reduce him to a pile of smoking ash, and failed dismally to find one.

Harriet did not return to the house immediately. She told herself that she needed to regain some measure of composure before she faced her grandfather's hawk gaze again, and responded to the inevitable inquisition.

Yet it wasn't Gregory Flint, or his possible reaction to recent events, which occupied the forefront of her mind as she made a long slow circuit of the lawns. And for once the gardens she knew and loved were not having their usual soothing effect.

Because Roan Zandros was getting in the way. How dared he look at her—speak to her like that? she asked herself furiously, defensively, especially when he'd had the unmitigated gall to appear at Gracemead uninvited and unwanted—a blatant intruder in her private and beloved world.

Well, she would have to teach him, and pretty damn quick, that his interference was unwarranted and unappreciated. Maybe a clause in the contract was needed, actually forbidding his return to Gracemead under any pretext.

He had to learn his place in their arrangement, and cosy visits were not on the agenda. Not now, and definitely not in the future.

She found her grandfather in the drawing room pouring sherry. He turned and looked at her, brows raised enquiringly. 'You're alone?'

'Why, yes.' She smiled brightly. 'I turned out to be not much of a guide, so Roan's conducting his own tour.'

He handed her a glass of her favourite *fino*, and gestured her to take a seat on the sofa facing his armchair. 'You and your fiancé haven't quarrelled already, I hope.'

'Of course not,' she denied swiftly. *Too swiftly?*

'Because it occurred to me that you were a little taken aback to find him here,' Gregory Flint went on. 'I hope it wasn't the subject of a disagreement between you.'

Harriet shrugged, trying for rueful amusement. 'You don't miss a thing, do you, darling?'

'I try not to, my dear.'

'Well, to be honest, I was a little miffed when I realised he'd stolen my thunder.' Harriet turned it into a faintly wistful confession. 'And I so much wanted to be the one to break the news to you about our engagement.'

'I'm quite sure you did.' There was a dry note in his voice, which did not escape her.

'Not that it really matters,' she added hastily. 'Just as long as you approve of my choice.'

'Let's say that I find him a most interesting young man,' Mr Flint said after a pause. 'He tells me you met through his work.'

The exact nature of the encounter still had the power to make her grind her teeth, and her smile was taut. 'We did indeed,' she said. 'And it made an unforgettable impression on me.'

'So I gather.' He leaned back in his armchair. 'You feel, then, that he has real talent?'

'Yes.' At least she could be totally honest about that. 'Yes, I do. He has this amazing use of colour—and emotion.'

'And will that earn him sufficient money to support a wife— and a family?'

Well, he'd slipped that in under the wire, Harriet thought, her heartbeat quickening. 'I believe so,' she said. 'And anyway, I shan't be giving up my career.'

'Ah,' he said. 'But has it occurred to you that your future husband might have his own ideas?'

Why—what's he been saying? That was the question she was burning to ask. Instead she said lightly, 'Even so, we still have to be practical.'

'And you've always been that, Harriet.' Pensively, Gregory Flint studied the colour of his sherry. 'Finding solutions to any problems that presented themselves—fighting to stay ahead of the game. Quite admirable in a great many ways.

'So, I find it all the more surprising that it should be the emotion in Roan's work that has appealed to you, instead of its strictly commercial aspect. Heart instead of head for once. I congratulate you.'

He raised his glass. 'And I drink to your future happiness, dear child. But at the same time I find myself wondering if you know—if you really know—exactly what you're taking on.'

Harriet was still digesting that when Roan rejoined them, smiling pleasantly, his voice unruffled as he praised the gardens with obvious sincerity. And in a way that revealed he knew what he was talking about, she registered sourly.

But gardening couldn't occupy the entire conversation, and throughout dinner she felt as if she was treading barefoot through broken glass, waiting for her grandfather to ask something—some question about their relationship—some small personal detail that she'd flounder over in humiliating self-betrayal. And what a wide range that offered, she thought.

But she eventually become aware that Roan was manipulating the conversation, quietly and skilfully, moving it away from topics about which she was woefully and dangerously ignorant to more general subjects.

And that under this guise he was actually imparting information—telling her stuff that, by rights, she should already know about the man she was to marry.

For one thing, he mentioned that his father was still alive, and living in Greece, adding casually that his parents had separated while he was a small child, but not elaborating any further.

But when he said that his late mother had been Vanessa Abbot, the celebrated miniaturist, Harriet had to struggle not to let her jaw drop.

Gregory Flint was clearly equally astonished, but all he said was, 'That explains the artistic talent my granddaughter so admires. Once again, as the saying goes, the apple doesn't fall far from the tree.'

But was it true? Harriet wondered grimly, observing from under lowered lashes the sardonic twist of Roan's lips as he raised his glass and drank. Because she wouldn't put it past her grandfather to check. And would his other claim to have attended a famous English public school stand up to scrutiny either?

Oh, God, she thought, seething, there would have been no need for any of this nonsense if Roan Zandros had simply—stayed away and minded his own business.

As dinner ended, Harriet heard with relief Roan accepting her grandfather's surprisingly genial challenge to a game of chess. Wonderful game, she thought, played mainly in silence, which suited her just fine, because she wasn't sure that her nervous system could stand any more questionable revelations.

She waited until they were well settled with their brandy over the ivory and ebony board, then smothered a manufactured yawn.

'Oh dear,' she said sweetly. 'I'm afraid my hectic week is catching up with me. If you'll both excuse me, I think I'll have an early night.'

She blew a smiling kiss aimed somewhere between the pair of them, and headed out of the drawing room, longing only to reach the safety of her room.

But as she reached the foot of the stairs she heard Roan say her name, and looked round, alarmed, to see him closing the drawing room door behind him before walking towards her across the hall.

'What do you want?' she demanded defensively.

'I am merely obeying instructions, *matia mou*.' He shrugged, his eyes glinting in amusement. 'Your grandfather has sent me to bid you a romantic goodnight in private, while he considers his next move.'

'Well, consider it done,' she said curtly. 'And I only hope you can remember the details of the rubbish you've been talking over dinner, because he has the memory of an elephant. Whatever possessed you to come out with all that stuff?'

'Because I thought it was what he wanted to hear, Harriet *mou*,' he drawled. 'A reassurance that you were not throwing yourself away on—nobody.'

'Just a liar and a conman, instead,' Harriet said scornfully. 'But maybe that's all to the good. At least he won't be able to oppose the divorce when I confess tearfully how you betrayed and deceived me. In essence, made utter fools of us both.'

He gave her a meditative look. 'You don't think that is a little harsh—on someone who wants only your happiness?'

'Except that Grandfather and I don't agree on what that involves.' She paused. 'And let me remind you that I've paid for your acquiescence, Mr Zandros, not your opinion.'

'Perhaps you are the one who needs a reminder, Harriet *mou*,' he said softly. Without warning his hands descended on her shoulders, jerking her towards him, and before she could utter any kind of protest his mouth took hers in a long, hard, and arrogantly deliberate kiss.

She tried to struggle—to free herself—but the arms holding her were far too strong, and determined. She could hardly breathe—let alone speak—or think.

She began to feel giddy, tiny coloured sparks dancing behind her closed eyelids, as the relentless pressure of his lips went on—and on—carrying her into some dark and swirling eternity.

And then—as suddenly as it had begun—it was over, and Roan was stepping back, putting her at arm's length, his dark eyes watching her unsmilingly.

Harriet stood, swaying slightly, lifting shaking fingers to touch the ravaged contours of her mouth, her mind blurred—incredulous. She tried to say something, but no words would come.

'Is that acquiescent enough for you, *kyria*?' His voice seemed to reach her across some vast wasteland. 'I would not wish you to feel you were wasting your money.' He added harshly, 'Now, go to bed, and I hope you enjoy your dreams.'

And he turned and went back across the wide hall into the drawing room, leaving her dazed and trembling. Aware only that, in some strange way, she was suddenly more utterly alone than she'd ever been in her life before.

CHAPTER FIVE

IT HAD not been passion. Even someone as woefully inexperienced as Harriet could appreciate that. On the contrary, it had been, she thought, more of a calculated insult. She'd provoked him. He'd responded. And that was it.

Her mouth still felt faintly swollen from his unwanted attentions, she realised with disgust, and there was a strange ache in her breasts—the result of them being crushed against the hardness of his chest, no doubt.

A sensation she would give a great deal to forget, she thought, drawing a quick sharp breath. No one had ever—handled her like that before. She'd made deadly sure of that. It was the stuff her worst nightmares were made of.

But on this occasion she hadn't seen it coming, and therefore she hadn't been able to take the evasive action she'd brought to a fine art.

But matters couldn't rest there. That was obvious. So, in the morning she would have to do—something. But what?

Because, technically, it was already morning, and, even though she'd been lying there for hours, staring sleeplessly into the darkness, she still hadn't the least idea how to deal with the situation.

The obvious answer, of course, was to abandon the whole idea. Tell him she'd changed her mind and the deal was off. That there would be no wedding.

And therefore no Gracemead either, she thought, pain twisting inside her, because then she'd have to confess to her grandfather and reap the inevitable consequences. He would naturally demand an explanation for the collapse of her 'engagement', and there was no way she'd be able to hide the truth from him for long, even if Roan kept his mouth shut, which was by no means certain.

And that meant she'd also have to bear with Gramps's anger and disappointment over her attempt to deceive him. And, quite rightly, he'd never trust her again.

She could feel the sting of tears in her eyes—taste their acridity in her throat.

I should never have started this, she told herself in desolation. Because nothing—nothing is worth this kind of pain, and that bastard was quite right about that, damn him.

What was more, that same bastard would still be around to be dealt with, she reminded herself grimly. She'd have to fulfil her commitments to him. The deal with the gallery was already set up, so there was nothing she could do about that. But she guessed she'd have to pay him the agreed lump sum too, if only to make him go away.

But perhaps that was exactly what he wanted her to do, she thought, sitting up suddenly as if she'd been jabbed by a cattle prod. Maybe he'd figured out exactly how to push her to the limit, and that—travesty of a kiss had simply been a deliberate ploy to get her to cry off.

In that way he could avoid keeping his part of the bargain, and walk away with everything he wanted. Leaving her plans in ruins yet again.

Just a conman after all, completing his 'sting', she thought, aware of an odd stir of disappointment.

But only if she let him, she rallied herself. And maybe he hadn't taken that into his calculations while he was—mauling her.

Well, now it was time to demonstrate that she was made of stronger stuff.

Because she wouldn't let him win. There was too much at stake for her to draw back now, however compelling the reason might seem.

So, she would treat the entire episode as some—temporary aberration, she planned, her heart racing. Dismiss it lightly as an irrelevance. Make it clear that all she wanted was his name on a marriage certificate, following which he could—paint himself into a corner for all she cared.

At the same time, she had to admit that he'd forced her to become altogether too aware of him as a man, rather than a signature on the dotted line she required. In fact, if she was honest, he'd been an irritation—an all-singing, all-dancing thorn in her side—from the moment they'd met.

And now flesh and blood instead of the obedient, malleable figment of her imagination—and her will. And she found the reality—disturbing. She'd needed a stranger who would remain strictly a stranger, and suddenly it had become—up close and personal. Dear God, he was here—sleeping in one of the guest rooms. Or awake and thinking—what?

But I can't let it matter, she thought, staring round the moonlit room. This is my home. It's my own place—the only security I've ever known, and I won't let him take it away from me.

So, I'll just have to be more careful in future.

When she arrived, heavy-eyed and faintly jittery, in the breakfast room next morning, it was to find Roan in sole occupancy, finishing off what appeared to be a substantial plate of bacon, mushrooms and scrambled egg.

'*Kalimera.*' He got politely to his feet. 'Your grandfather asked me to say that he will be breakfasting in his room today.'

'Oh.' Harriet poured cereal into a bowl and added milk. She frowned. 'He's not ill, is he?'

'Not at all.' As she sat down, Roan resumed his own seat, then poured her a cup of freshly brewed coffee, and handed it to her. A civility which she accepted with gritted teeth. 'I believe he thinks we might appreciate some time alone together.'

'How very misguided of him,' she returned coolly. 'How did the chess go?'

'It ended in stalemate.' His mouth twisted. 'Neither of us seemed able to find the other's weak point.'

'Grandfather doesn't have one,' she said. 'I suggest you play your games elsewhere in future.'

'Your early night,' he said slowly, 'does not seem to have sweetened your temper, Harriet *mou*. Is it possible you have changed your mind about marrying me?'

Dream on, she told him silently.

Aloud, 'Certainly not,' she said briskly. 'Unlikely as it may seem, you appear to have ingratiated yourself with my grandfather, so once you've signed the pre-nuptial agreement the ceremony can go ahead as planned, and with his blessing.'

'Although not in his presence,' Roan said quietly. 'He told me he does not approve of civil ceremonies. They smack, he says, too much of the rubber stamp.'

She gasped. 'You mean you invited him?'

'I thought he might wish to give you away, Harriet *mou*.'

'Well, thank goodness he didn't,' she said roundly. 'It could have caused all kinds of problems. As it is, we can just—seal the deal, and go our separate ways.' She offered him a small chilly smile. 'I'll be in touch.'

There was a silence then he said, too courteously, 'I live for the moment.' He rose to his feet. 'And now I must tear myself from you, Harriet *mou*. A cab is coming to take me to the station.' He paused. 'You need not accompany me to the door. We can let your grandfather assume we said a tender goodbye to each other in private.'

'You're all consideration,' she said tautly. 'But I always prefer to see visitors off the premises.'

His brows lifted. 'You are not very trusting, my sweet one.'

'Small wonder,' she said. 'And please don't call me by that ridiculous name. I am neither sweet nor yours.'

He looked at her for a long moment, and she felt her heartbeat quicken involuntarily—uncontrollably.

But when he spoke, there was no hint of anger in his voice. 'It is not easy to please you, Harriet. But—I shall continue to try just the same.' He then added quietly, 'Now, finish your breakfast in peace.'

And he went, leaving Harriet sitting at the table, staring at absolutely nothing, her cereal uneaten and unwanted.

It would have to be the beige linen shift again, Harriet realised as she prepared to dress for her wedding. It was either that or one of her innumerable shapeless black trouser suits. She had nothing else in her wardrobe.

And the dress was freshly laundered, she thought, regarding herself critically in the mirror. It looked clean and crisp enough.

Yet it occurred to her, uneasily, that maybe she should have stretched a point and bought something to be married in. Not a wedding dress, as such. Nothing white or—or virginal. That was going too far. But something simple and pretty that would also do service on summer evenings, and during weekends down at Gracemead.

And perhaps she should have tied her hair back for once with something more elegant than an elastic band.

But why am I beating myself up about this? she asked herself with impatience. It's not as if it's a real wedding, or I'm a real bride. And Roan will probably turn up in jeans anyway.

Nevertheless, she felt a vague dissatisfaction as she took a final look at herself, and left the bedroom.

She'd ordered a cab to take her to the register office, but it wasn't due for another five minutes, so she filled the time writing Roan's cheque, and putting it in an envelope with one of her office compliment slips. After a moment's thought, she took the slip out again, and wrote on it, 'With every good wish for the future.'

The personal touch, she thought, her mouth twisting.

Then she sat on the edge of the sofa feeling oddly lost, her calm, pared-down environment for once failing to soothe her.

Not that there was anything to worry about. It was all going according to plan. And Roan had gone to her lawyer's office and signed the pre-nuptial agreement without a murmur.

'Although I feared the worst,' Isobel had told her. 'He turned up with his own legal eagle—a guy called Jack Maxwell who's pretty high-powered—and they spent quite some time going through it, line by line. I hope we haven't forgotten anything.'

She'd paused. 'I also hope you know what you're doing, Harry. What do you really know about this man, except that he's broke and gorgeous?'

'I know he's a brilliant artist,' Harriet returned a touch defensively. 'That his mother was a well-known painter too, who met his father while she was on holiday in Greece. Apparently he's involved in the Greek tourist industry, or so Roan told Gramps over their chess game. Which means that the old boy probably owns a taverna, and the son didn't fancy a life waiting on tables. And he can hardly be blamed for that.'

'No,' Isobel agreed. 'He didn't seem too thrilled, by the way, with the clause barring him from Gracemead and any further contact with your grandfather.'

'Pure safety measure.' Harriet paused. 'But he needs the money too much to make a fuss.'

'Really?' Isobel asked sceptically. 'I reckon he could earn more by renting himself out in the afternoons.' She hesitated. 'You're taking too much on trust here, Harry. Why not put the thing on hold while I make some proper enquiries about him?'

'You wouldn't require background checks if I was—hiring a decorator,' Harriet argued. 'Well, the same principle applies. He does the job he's paid for, then walks. It's that simple.'

Only, now the day had come, the situation seemed marginally more complex.

God knew, she'd never intended to be married, but on the rare occasions when the thought had crossed her mind, she'd not visualised a wedding like this. Or imagined that after the ceremony she'd be going back to work as if nothing had happened.

But then no bridegroom in her imagination had ever resembled Roan Zandros either, she reminded herself wryly, as the buzzer sounded, signalling the arrival of her taxi.

As she walked into the building that housed the register office, she found herself half hoping that Roan wouldn't be there. That his married blonde lady had raised some insuperable objection to the plan.

But that was defeatist thinking, she told herself, just when she was on the brink of achieving exactly what she wanted.

And of course he was there, in the waiting room, wearing, she noticed instantly, another elegant dark suit, with a white rose in his buttonhole.

He must have a friend with an extensive wardrobe, Harriet thought, drawing a deep breath as she made herself walk forward. But neither of the men waiting with him was tall enough. Although the pair of them were equally smartly garbed, and also wearing white roses.

Very festive, she thought, biting her lip. Whereas she didn't have as much as a daisy to carry—a point that clearly wasn't lost on anyone present. Making her feel as if she was having one of those ghastly dreams where you found yourself attending a Buckingham Palace garden party in your underwear.

Making her wish suddenly—ridiculously—that she had tried harder, instead of dressing down in her usual anonymous manner. Taken the trouble to have her hair done, and fitted in a professional make-up and manicure.

That just for once she'd turned herself into a girl a man might genuinely want to marry, so that they'd be looking at her now with admiration rather than blank astonishment. Because, however little it might feel like it, she was a bride, and this was her wedding day.

One of Roan's companions came over to her. He was stockily built, with sandy hair, and a square-chinned good-looking face currently marred by a faintly inimical expression.

'Good morning, Miss Flint.' He spoke without particular warmth. 'I'm Jack Maxwell, and this is my colleague Carl Winston. We're here as witnesses.'

He looked more like a rugby player than a tough lawyer, Harriet thought with surprise.

He went on, 'Perhaps you might like to fulfil the financial part of your agreement with my client now? He's authorised me to accept the money on his behalf.'

Surprised, she glanced at Roan, who nodded unsmilingly, then handed over the envelope, wishing she hadn't included that stupid message. Wishing all kinds of confused things but principally that she was anywhere but here.

Or in this other room, across the corridor, facing a grey-haired woman in a smart blue suit, repeating the words she was being asked to say, and holding out her hand so that Roan could place a gold ring on her third finger.

And then, so quickly, it was all over, and they were outside in the sunlight, but no one was throwing confetti or rose petals, nor was there a car to drive away in with her new husband, or any well-wishers waving and pointing cameras.

Nor, thankfully, had anyone suggested that they should kiss the bride, least of all the groom.

There was a difficult silence, then Jack Maxwell said, 'Well, friends, I move that we find a bar, and some lunch.'

Harriet's lips were parting to tell him she had to go to the office when she realised, just in time, that the invitation was not intended for her.

But if they imagined she was just going to slink away, as if she was ashamed of what she'd done, they could think again, she decided, lifting her chin.

She approached Roan, smiling brightly. 'Goodbye, Mr Zandros.' Her voice was crystal-clear. 'It's been a pleasure to do business with you.' She tugged off her wedding ring and handed it to him. 'A small souvenir of the transaction,' she added, and walked away without looking back.

It was not one of Harriet's better afternoons. It seemed to consist of numerous small, irritating tasks that needed lengthy phone calls to resolve them, and by the end of the day she still wasn't convinced she'd achieved very much. Nor had she been given a chance to look at the Midlands project.

Worst of all, as she was leaving, Tony asked her to call at Hayford House on her way home, to listen to complaints about the house-keeping and maintenance service from some of the tenants.

And there were plenty of them. She listened patiently, making notes about communal areas left uncleaned and untidy, the unmended tumble dryer in the basement laundry, the replacement door chains not yet fitted, the unsatisfactory garbage collection, plus assorted dripping taps and faulty ballcocks.

'We're sorry to make a fuss, but we have raised these points before.' Mrs Guthrie, an elderly widow, smiled apologetically. 'Mr Audley was charming, but obviously a very busy young man, so our little domestic concerns may have slipped his mind.'

Well, thank you, Tony, Harriet thought furiously. You might have warned me I was clearing up one of Jon Audley's messes. And in the morning I shall send that—charmer—an e-mail that will make his nose bleed.

As she went home, still seething, it occurred to her that she'd been sidelined a fair bit over the past couple of weeks—assigned to cope with details rather than the big picture. Or was she just being paranoid?

Whatever, she needed to regain some of the ground she appeared to have lost, or at this rate she might find herself being sent out at lunchtimes to pick up the sandwiches.

Thinking of food reminded her of how little she'd had to eat that day, and that even less awaited her in the fridge at home.

Perhaps it was just hunger that was prompting this uneasy, restless feeling, and a good meal would have her firing on all cylinders again. Maybe even celebrating her victory over Gracemead, which had somehow become relegated to the back of her mind.

She stopped off at her local branch of a popular restaurant chain, where she ordered herself a fillet steak with fries and all the trimmings, including a glass of red wine, and followed this up with a slice of lemon meringue pie served with thick cream, and two cups of strong coffee.

She felt more contented when she arrived back at the flat. And she'd be better still once she'd taken a relaxing bath. She might even feel like tackling her report on the tenants' grievances, to present to Tony in the morning. Make him see she was a force to be reckoned with.

The sunset glow was already fading from the sky, so she closed the blinds in the living room and lit a couple of lamps before making for her bathroom with a sigh of anticipation, discarding her clothing as she went.

It was almost an hour later when, dried and scented, she put on a new pair of peach satin pyjamas, and began slowly to brush her newly freed chestnut hair back from her face, enjoying the luxurious sensation of the soft fabric gliding against her skin as her arm moved slowly and rhythmically.

Relishing the perfect order of her environment, with her room tidied and the bed turned down. Looking forward to the peace of the evening ahead of her, and the chance to feel totally relaxed at last.

Except…

She paused, frowning a little, wondering if she'd acquired a new and noisy neighbour, because she was sure she'd heard a door opening and closing not too far away.

In fact, altogether too near for comfort.

For a moment Harriet stood motionless, hardly breathing, as she listened, telling herself it was pure imagination. That it couldn't possibly be her own door, because she'd locked up securely, as always.

But for the first time Harriet regretted there was no phone extension in the bedroom. Wished she hadn't left her mobile in her brief-case by the sofa.

Not, of course, that there was anything to worry about. One of this apartment block's advantages was a concierge service, and no one ever got past George, an ex-Royal Marine. The events of the day had left her edgy, that was all.

Just the same...

Taking a deep breath, she put down her brush, and trod barefoot to the doorway which led into her living room.

Where she stopped abruptly, gasping as if a monstrous hand had descended on her ribcage, squeezing the breath from her lungs.

'*Kalispera*, Harriet *mou*,' Roan Zandros said softly, and smiled at her in the lamplight.

He was standing in the centre of the room, still dressed pretty much as he'd been at the wedding, except that his tie had gone, leaving his shirt open at the throat, and he had a small but serviceable rucksack slung across one shoulder.

'What are you doing here?' She was proud of her voice, cool, uncompromising and steady as a rock. Especially as every pulse in her body was going suddenly crazy—thudding out a tattoo—a call to arms. When her legs were shaking so badly she had to resist an impulse to lean against the doorframe for support.

'Where else should I be?' He dropped the rucksack on to the black kid sofa, following it with his jacket. The dark eyes challenged her. 'We were married today, or had you forgotten?'

'We went through a ceremony, certainly,' she returned curtly. He must have got her address from the pre-nuptial agreement, which he was now flouting, of course, she thought frantically. And swallowed. 'How did you get in here, anyway?'

'The concierge loaned me the spare key.' He paused. 'I am to return it in the morning.'

The precise implications of that dried her throat to sand.

This couldn't be happening. He couldn't be here, invading her privacy, intruding on her personal space, not when he'd promised—*promised*...

And seeing her off-guard, she realised, as no one was allowed to. And when—dear God—her only covering was a thin layer of satin.

Something that was not lost on him either, as she felt his eyes travelling slowly over her from the top of her head down to her bare toes. Saw his smile widen.

But she couldn't waste time worrying about her clothing, or lack of it. The important thing was to keep her head, behave with dignity and decision—and get him out of there.

She rallied her wits and her voice. 'That's news to me.'

'That there is a spare key?'

'No, that George simply hands it out to passing strangers. He may well lose his job over this.'

'Why—for bringing together a man and his bride on their wedding night?' He shook his head. 'I don't think so.'

Wedding night...

Harriet's throat tightened. 'All the same, I'd prefer you to return the key to him—and go.'

'Except that tonight it will not be your preferences that matter, but mine,' he retorted with equal incisiveness. 'And I mean to stay.'

Breathing was becoming a problem—something she dared not let him know. She said with faint huskiness, 'If this is some crude and taste-less attempt to be funny, then it's failed. Now, for the last time, get out.'

'But I am not joking.' Roan began slowly to remove the cufflinks from his shirt. 'Nor am I leaving.'

Their eyes met. His, cool and unswerving. Hers—appalled.

'Because I am here to claim my marital rights, *agapi mou*,' he went on softly. 'One of the few options left to me by the draconian contract you insisted I sign.'

He paused. 'And something of which I intend to take full advan-tage.'

His words dropped like fragments of ice into the taut, frightened silence that seemed to enfold her.

She made herself speak, her voice strained. 'I—I think you must have gone mad. Our agreement specifies that we—live separately. You knew that—accepted it.'

He said, quite gently, 'I agreed not to share your roof. But if you also meant to deny me your body, then you should have stated as much. Only, you did not, Harriet *mou*, so I am breaking no promise.'

That was why he'd spent so much time at Isobel's office going over the damned thing, she thought. Because he'd been looking for a loophole—some way of getting back at her.

Fool, she castigated herself silently. Bloody imbecile. How could you have allowed such a basic omission to slip past?

Because, she thought, it had never occurred to her there was any possibility that he might—that he'd ever want...

And she wouldn't believe it now, she told herself, rallying her defences. He had some other agenda. That had to be it.

She said stonily, 'This is nonsense. I made it perfectly clear that I had no intention of being your wife—in that way.'

'Yet you did not bother to consider what my own intentions might be.' He paused, allowing her to digest that. 'However, I have no plans to move in permanently, Harriet *mou*,' he added silkily, glancing round him at the plain walls, pale wood and streamlined black furniture. 'I find the ambience a little stark for my tastes, therefore I shall just be spending the night.'

He dropped his cufflinks on to the coffee table, and started to unbutton his shirt.

He smiled at her. 'So, let us hope that your bed offers more in the way of comfort than your living room. I look forward to finding out.'

CHAPTER SIX

HARRIET felt as if she'd turned to stone. She stared at him—casually undressing in front of her—her mind in freefall. She could, of course, step backwards and shut her bedroom door against him, but that wouldn't keep him out permanently, and the essential key to the lock was—elsewhere. In some cupboard, probably, or some drawer. My God, she didn't even know. Couldn't think. And because all the furniture was fitted, there wasn't even a chair or a tallboy she could use as a barricade.

And, as he'd demonstrated on that first encounter in his studio, and since, he was infinitely stronger than she was. If she tried to fight him off physically, she would undoubtedly lose.

Although it couldn't be allowed to get to that point. After all, she'd been the prime mover in this situation, and somehow she had to reassert her dominance. Mentally, emotionally—and fast.

She swallowed. 'I think you must be—genuinely crazy,' she said. 'But please understand that I have absolutely no intention of sleeping with you.'

'So there is no problem,' he returned pleasantly. 'Because sleep does not feature on my list of priorities either.'

There was another terrible silence as she watched him shrug off his shirt, and toss it after his jacket. As she saw his hands move to the buckle of his belt...

She drew a deep, unsteady breath. 'That's quite enough. You— you can stop right there.'

Roan paused. 'Was there some clause in the agreement dictating what I wear in bed?' he wondered aloud, then shook his head. 'I don't remember it.'

'No clause,' she said hoarsely. 'Just—common decency, which you seem to lack. And if this is a ploy to get more money out of me, it won't work, even if you strip a dozen times. It was obviously stupid of me to imagine I could trust you,' she added bitingly. 'But I'm wiser now, and the marriage ends here and now.'

'Not yet, my unwilling wife,' he said softly. 'It is about to begin. I thought I had made that clear.'

Her stomach was churning wildly. 'Then let me also make something clear,' she rasped. 'I'll see you in court, Mr Zandros, before I give in to this kind of blackmail.'

'It should make a fascinating case.' He stood watching her, hands on hips. 'I can see the tabloid headlines now.' He paused. 'And imagine your grandfather's reaction to them, and the way you have tried to deceive him. I think you could say goodbye to your hopes of Gracemead, don't you?'

With every moment, her wonderful spacious room—her sanctuary—seemed to be shrinking, while increasing her acute awareness of him at the same time.

Somehow she had to redress the balance, she told herself desperately. Stop this whole impossible situation right now before it went too far—if it hadn't done so already.

It wasn't easy to keep him at a safe distance without making it too obvious that she was skirting round him, because the last thing she wanted was to seem nervous, but she managed it somehow. Difficult, as well, to try to appear dignified in spite of her flimsy pyjamas and bare feet as she crossed the living room, although she was heart-thuddingly conscious that she was still marginally more covered than he was.

She reached the door and stood beside it, her head held high, grasping the handle tightly in an attempt to disguise that her fingers were shaking.

'If you leave now,' she said, lifting her chin, 'and don't come back, then we—we'll forget this ever happened. If you don't, I shall call the police.'

'And say what?' he enquired mockingly. 'That you are a bride reluctant to lose your virginity to the husband you married this morning?'

She gasped. 'That is—a disgustingly arrogant assumption.'

'I assume nothing,' he said softly. 'I know I shall be the first. And I think the police would be fascinated by your complaint,' he went on. 'They might also charge you with wasting their valuable time. And don't attempt to buy them too, because that might prove truly misguided.'

He paused, allowing her to assimilate that. 'Also that door is locked, so stop making empty gestures, *matia mou*, and come here to me.'

'No.' Her fingers tightened convulsively on the door handle—the only solid object in a reeling world. 'I—I take back what I said just now. Everything I've said. Because I will pay you—I'll pay anything—if you'll just—go away. And leave me in peace.'

'Harriet,' he said gently. 'Today I took you as my wife. Tonight I take you as my woman, as I intended from the first. And, whatever you may think, it was never a question of money.'

'Then what?' Her voice was hoarse. 'Is this your idea of revenge, for my having—insulted your manhood in some way? Because you don't really want me, and you know it.'

He sighed. 'If I did not want you, *pedhi mou*, then, believe me, I would not be here. And maybe I was angry at first,' he went on grimly. 'Angry over your assumption that I must be for sale and would meekly accept this sterile bargain of yours at its face value.

'But I was not angry for long.' He smiled at her. 'Because the first time I touched you, I knew there was a body to be desired under those shapeless garments you favour, in public at least.' His dark gaze lingered on the swell of her breasts, then travelled slowly down to the indentation of her waist and the supple outline of her hips and thighs.

'And my instinct was correct,' he added softly. 'You look enchanting. That is a good colour for you, my sweet one. It adds warmth to your skin, even when you are not blushing.'

'Kindly keep your dubious compliments to yourself,' Harriet said raggedly. 'And, as I've already told you, I'm neither sweet nor yours.'

'Not yet, perhaps,' Roan agreed. 'But I am hoping your attitude may soften once we become more intimately acquainted.'

'Then go on hoping,' she said fiercely. 'Because in reality you're trying to force yourself on someone who doesn't want you.'

'Are you so sure that is how you feel?' Roan questioned softly. 'I would say the jury is still out.'

'Then you'd be totally wrong.' She conjured up the image of the blonde she'd encountered at his studio. 'For God's sake, how many women do you need to have?'

He tutted reprovingly, his eyes dancing. 'What a question for a bride to put to her husband. But, since you ask, I find one at a time suits me perfectly.' He grinned at her. 'My tastes are not yet so jaded that they require—additional stimulation.'

He walked to her without hurry, detaching her clutching fingers from the door handle quietly and without force.

She stared up at him, her eyes dilating. 'Roan.' She was hardly aware she'd used his name. 'Roan—please. Don't do this—I—I beg you.' Her voice was a whisper.

'And what is—"this" that scares you so, Harriet *mou*?' He shook his head. 'I don't think you even know.'

But you're wrong, she thought. *So very wrong. Because I know from my childhood—from my mother going from man to man, hoping, seeking the impossible. I remember all the soft words in each beginning—the promises 'Trust me…' 'I'll never leave you…'*

The sounds in the night from the other side of the wall that I was too young to understand.

And then the other sounds—the shouting, the crashing, the slamming of doors. The silences that were somehow the loudest of all. And then the weeping, the quiet, terrible sobbing of failure and desolation. Before someone else came along with more sweet talk, more promises, and the whole cycle began again.

And I swore I would never let that happen to me. That I would not be like her—dependent on the sexual whim of some man.

That, instead, I would be my own woman, answering only to myself. And my body would always be my own…

Thought it, but did not say it as Roan's hands came down on her at last.

She was trembling openly now, her anger commingled with fear, as he drew her towards him, and she braced her hands against his chest, twisting wildly, striving to break free.

'Let me go,' she gasped. 'Let me go, damn you. Oh, God, I'll never forgive you for this. Never!'

'Never is a very long time, *agapi mou*,' he told her softly. 'When all you have to endure is one night. Now, be still.'

Just as she'd feared, he controlled her frantic struggles with effortless ease, pinioning her slender wrists behind her with one hand, while with the other he cupped her chin, raising her face so that her tightly clamped, rebellious mouth was his for the taking.

And not just her mouth, she realised with agonised humiliation. Her vain attempts to release herself had resulted instead in freeing some of the silk buttons on her pyjama jacket, so that her rounded breasts were now bare to the smouldering heat of his dark gaze.

He said in a harsh whisper, 'You are—so beautiful.'

The hand clamping her wrists in the small of her back propelled her forward, bringing her into sudden, intimate contact with the hard wall of his chest, so that the dark springing hair grazed the dusky rose of her nipples, making them lift and harden in a swift, shamed pleasure she was unable to control or deny.

And then he kissed her.

But if the last time had been punishment, this was entirely different. And, she realised, infinitely more dangerous.

Because Roan's lips were warm and ineffably gentle as they caressed hers, his mission, this time, to persuade—and arouse. Which was the last thing she'd expected, or wanted.

She needed him to be rough—even brutal—she thought feverishly, so that she could feed her resistance to him—her loathing and contempt for this—unbelievable treachery.

So that she could teach him, in one icy lesson, that he would get nothing from her but her bleak and unswerving indifference—the only weapon now left in her admittedly futile armoury—forcing him to leave, disappointed with his hollow victory, and never come back.

But she knew now, in this first moment, how right it was to be afraid of him. And not because she feared the violence of a forced surrender. Instead it was the coaxing insistence of his mouth as it moved on hers that scared her. The way her traitorous senses were reacting to the texture of his skin, the warmth of his body penetrating the little clothing she had left, and the unbelievable intoxication of his unique male scent as his arms tightened round her.

And, worst of all, the hardness of him against her thighs, the stark proof that he did indeed want her. Because this explicit power of his arousal was somehow triggering an instant and shaming response from her—the kind of meltdown in her most intimate self that she'd never envisaged in her whole life. The scalding, physical rush of what could only be animal desire.

Except it couldn't be true, because she was immune—wasn't she? Had based her whole life on her iron resolve to remain celibate. But it was simple to claim immunity when there was no temptation. She could see that now when it was—almost too late.

When the firewall she'd built around herself was crumbling, engulfed by a flame she hadn't known existed, but which she had to fight—and extinguish before it became a fire.

Battling, she realised, for self-respect, as well as self-preservation, and the safe, solitary future which she could not—would not relinquish.

But, in that same instant, she realised that her hands were no longer imprisoned in his grasp, and that Roan was taking his mouth from hers and looking down at her, the dark gaze not arrogant in triumph, as she might have expected, but hooded, questioning.

Harriet stared back, some female instinct telling her urgently that it was still not too late. That somehow—for some inexplicable reason—she was being offered a choice. That if she said no this time, he would listen, and, in spite of everything that had gone before, he would not force the issue. And that he would let her go.

And all she had to do was speak.

No was such a small word, she thought, and so simple to use that even very young children could manage it. And it was a lifeline. The only one…

She drew a deep breath, framing the negative clearly and concisely in her head, but no sound emerged except the faintest of sighs.

Not even when he began to touch her, his fingers light as they stroked her cheek and moved slowly downwards, teasing the lobe of her ear, then lingering on the leap and quiver of her pulse, before slipping under her collar to explore the angles and hollows of her throat and shoulder.

Nor when she realised his other hand was resting, without force, on the curve of her hip, and she would only have to step backwards to detach herself—even move out of range altogether.

So why was she was simply standing there—mute, unmoving and half undressed? Looking at him, oh, God, as if she was—waiting…

And in that moment Roan bent his head, his mouth finding her parted lips with renewed and sensuous urgency, his tongue gliding against hers in deliberate demand.

Harriet found she was suddenly quivering, as if her skin had become imbued—sensitised with a thousand tiny electrical charges, coming to life with treacherous vibrancy as his kiss deepened endlessly. The person she'd been an hour ago—the cool, ambitious career woman—no longer seemed to exist.

In her place was a creature she didn't recognise, who was allowing a man, for the first time in her life, to explore her mouth with passionate sexuality. And that was only the first of the demands that would be made of her.

Because, at the same time, his hand was moving downwards to the warm, proud lift of her breast, where it lingered, shaping the soft swell with his palm while his thumb delicately traced the erect peak in a caress that pierced her to the core of her being.

'Oh, God.' The words came choking from her tight throat. 'I can't—please—*please*…'

But when his hand moved, it was only to release the remaining buttons of the satin jacket and push it from her shoulders, before running his fingers gently, lightly, over her back and down her spine, making her arch against him involuntarily so that the steely pressure of his body seemed already to be invading the damp, aching heat between her thighs.

Making her gasp into his mouth as, still kissing her, Roan lifted her into his arms and carried her across the living area, and into the lamplit bedroom beyond.

Throwing back the covers, he put her down on the bed, then straightened, and she heard the rasp of his zip as he prepared to remove the remainder of his clothing.

She said in a voice that didn't belong to her, 'Please—turn off the light.'

'So that you don't have to look at me?' he asked softly. 'Or so that I cannot look at you? Either way, it is not going to happen. Tonight you will need all your senses, *matia mou*.'

'You're vile,' she whispered, with a shadow of her former fierceness. 'You disgust me.'

He said laconically, 'Tell me that tomorrow.'

And then he was beside her, taking her tense, trembling body in his arms and holding her close to his warm, lithe strength. Confronting her with the reality of his naked presence in her bed.

He said softly, 'Don't fight me, Harriet *mou*. Whatever you may believe, I can be patient. And I am not going to hurt you.'

Any bitter response she might have planned was instantly stifled by his kiss, his mouth deeply searching, the play of his tongue against hers an irresistibly sensual challenge.

Then his lips moved slowly downwards, nibbling gently at the column of her neck, questing the hollows at the base of her throat, the fragile skin beneath her slender arms, and in the curve of her elbows.

Lashes veiling her eyes, she moved restively, her quickening breath sighing through her parted lips, as his lean fingers moulded and caressed the scented fullness of her breasts, then moved down to the waistband of her remaining garment to unfasten the single button and ease the whispering satin over her hips and down, so that she too was naked under the intensity of his dark eyes.

No one had ever seen her even half undressed before, or not since her early childhood, she thought frantically. And certainly no man—ever…

Her face burning, she tried to roll away, desperately covering herself with her hands, but he drew her back to him, gently but inexorably.

'You are too beautiful to hide yourself,' he told her softly. 'Lovelier even than in my dreams of you. And when you blush, you become the colour of a rose all over, Harriet *mou*. Did you know that?' There was a smile in his voice, but no mockery now. Instead he sounded—almost tender. 'I wondered if it would be so.'

He kissed her again, slowly and ever more deeply, and, in spite of herself, Harriet knew she wanted to respond. That it was all she could do not to slide her arms round his neck, to clasp her hands at the back of his head and hold his mouth to hers, so that this warm, languid exploration might never stop. So that she could capture the feel—the taste of him and make them a prisoner of her senses for ever.

And hating him—even hating herself—didn't change a thing.

She thought, shivering, I can't let this happen. Dear God—I can't…

Only to realise the decision was no longer hers to make. And had not been so since the first caress of his mouth and hands. That she'd been defeated—overwhelmed by the treachery of her own senses. Caught in a trap of her own making. A trap she no longer had the will to escape.

When at last Roan raised his head, she was humiliated to hear herself give a tiny whimper. He murmured something in his own language, his voice husky and soothing as he bent to her again, stroking her heated skin with his fingertips. And where his hands touched, his lips followed, marking out their own voluptuous path on her shivering, aching flesh.

She could feel her body yielding helplessly to his caresses, inch by quivering inch, and knew that she'd already reached a brink she'd never known existed until that moment. And that beyond it was the unknown. The unimaginable—and the unimagined.

Then, as Roan began to kiss her breasts, she stopped thinking altogether, every atom of her awareness suddenly and shockingly focussed on this new and dizzyingly erotic sensation.

On how his tongue was stroking her nipples with such exquisite precision, teasing them to a delicious wantonness that was half pleasure, half pain. Or how the touch of his mouth felt like velvet against her skin.

At the same time his questing hands continued to drift downwards, outlining her small waist, then fanning outwards across the flatness of her stomach to trace the curve of her hips, and linger…

She moved restively under his touch, driven by some totally

carnal imperative, telling herself that he could not stop there, because she could not bear it. That she needed to know—everything, even if she was never able to forgive herself for this shameful capitulation.

Tomorrow could take care of itself, she thought. But tonight—ah, God—tonight…

And as if she'd spoken aloud, made some plea, Roan's fingers moved down, gliding with delicate finesse over the silken mound at the joining of her thighs, then beyond, parting her slender legs to explore without haste the slick molten core of her womanhood, and to penetrate it—gently but with heart-stopping exactitude.

Her already laboured breathing caught in her throat, her tiny sob one of utter yearning as her body arched towards him in an offering she could no longer deny.

'Patience, *agapi mou*. I have no wish to hurt you.' His whisper was ragged, but the slow, subtle movement of his fingers inside her was totally deliberate—completely certain. And exquisitely, irresistibly pleasurable, she realised. Triggering a series of small, unbelievable sensations, which she focussed on blindly—greedily, instinct telling her that there was more—so much more in waiting. If only she could reach…

Making her want it—all of it. And—suddenly, terrifyingly—all of him too.

And, as if he'd read her fainting thought, Roan's touch changed, deepened, became explicit, so that suddenly her last remnants of control were slipping away, as the pleasure altered too, as she felt, somewhere in the depths of her being, a faint almost intangible throbbing. As it intensified, taking her by storm, drawing her into some fierce upward spiral of delight. As she moaned and writhed, crying out as the spiral of feeling reached its culmination, and her body was suddenly convulsed, torn apart by sharp rhythmic spasms that somehow combined agony with rapture.

And sobbed her helpless joy against his mouth.

Afterwards, there was silence, broken only by the sound of her own torn and flurried breathing, as she lay, eyes closed, struggling to regain command of her dazed and bewildered senses—and the body which had so utterly betrayed her.

Hectically conscious that she was still lying in his arms, with his lips against her hair, and that every nerve-ending in her damp awakened flesh was still tingling in euphoria.

Yet knowing at the same time that nothing had changed, in spite of the response he'd forced from her. He was still the stranger—the predator—the cheat. The enemy she would never forgive for the loss of her sexual independence. She would not call it innocence.

She was only thankful that he'd said nothing. That she'd not been subjected to some jeering and hideously truthful comment about the ease of his conquest. Which, of course, was not over yet.

Eventually he released her, and she felt him move away to the edge of the bed. Hoped for one brief instant that he was content with the humiliation he'd already inflicted. Might be merciful, and not insist on taking his triumph to its ultimate conclusion.

Until she heard the faint crackle of a packet being torn open, and understood its significance with a sinking heart. Knowing that he only planned to spare her the danger of pregnancy.

Not a detail overlooked, she thought bitterly, recalling the smoothness of his dark face against her skin, and its musky fragrance, indicating that he'd even taken the trouble to shave before he came to her.

He drew her back into his arms once more, whispering her name, compelling her to the trembling awareness of the hardness of him, all that male strength and potency hotly aroused against her thighs, and demanding the access that would consummate their union. Another aspect of the physical reality of intimacy that she could only dread. Because it was another opportunity for self-betrayal.

As he bent to kiss her, she turned her face away abruptly, and felt him pause.

'Sulking, *matia mou*?' he asked softly, the dark eyes quizzical. 'Angry that you now know yourself better than you did?'

'Is that your excuse for your—revolting behaviour?' Her voice was small and husky. 'That you've taken me on some—journey of self-discovery? Well, thank you for nothing, you bastard.'

There was a silence, then Roan said evenly, 'Strangely, I was trying to make your initiation into womanhood slightly less of an ordeal, Harriet *mou*. But perhaps that was foolish of me, and I should have ignored your inexperience, and any discomfort it might cause, and simply—taken you.'

He added harshly, 'I shall not make the same mistake again.'

Almost before she realised what was happening, he pushed her back against the mattress, reaching almost negligently for a pillow to slot under her hips. Then, lifting himself over her, his clenched fists clamped to the bed on either side of her body, he entered her in one smooth, purposeful thrust, her body still too relaxed in the aftermath of recent pleasure to offer any resistance.

She gasped wordlessly, and he paused. 'Am I hurting you?'

'No.' Her voice was a thread.

And it was true, she realised, as Roan inclined his head in curt acknowledgement and began to move, asserting his initial mastery ever more deeply with each slow, rhythmic thrust of his lean hips.

True—because she wasn't in pain, but in—astonishment. Devastated at the ease of his possession—amazed that her untried, resentful body could have accepted—sheathed—such formidable sexual power so effortlessly.

And a million miles from the traumatic act of domination that she'd feared.

In fact, the controlled impetus of his body in hers was already having an effect she'd not allowed for—because she'd not known it could exist.

Had not dreamed the joining of their flesh, the restrained force of him inside her, could, against all expectation, prove to be more enticement than subjection.

Or that it could create these incredible new sensations—these aching impossible needs. Suggesting that it was not just her body that she was surrendering, but her mind too.

Because desire was unfurling deep inside her like the first petals of a spring flower in the warmth of the sun. But desire for more than this basic coupling that she'd brought upon herself. She wanted the intimacy of touch—his lips parting hers, his hands on her fevered skin. Needed his earlier tenderness to alleviate the raw passion of conquest.

But what chance was there, when he wasn't even looking at her, his face a bronze mask, his mouth hard? Surely there was—something she could do.

His skin wore a faint sheen of sweat, and she watched it as if mesmerised—wondering if it would feel as exquisitely, thrillingly silken as the hardness that was filling her—moving inside her. And how it would be if she allowed her hands—her lips—to find out for themselves.

Commonsense dictated that she should just lie quietly, letting him use her in any way he chose, so that it would be over, and she could be rid of him. Because what she needed was her life back—not something else to regret.

Yet the memory of the delight he'd given her only minutes before was still urgent in her mind, the longing to make these discoveries about him well-nigh irresistible, no matter how much she might despise herself later.

I have to know…

Eyes half closed, she yielded, lifting her hands and running them lightly up his arms to his shoulders, then along to the nape of his neck, mapping the superb grace of his bone structure, feeling the taut muscles clench under her lingering fingertips.

Aware that the imperative drive of his body had faltered. Arrested. That he was still poised above her, but unmoving, the dark eyes watching her under sharply drawn brows.

'Did I do something wrong?' She was bewildered, even mortified that she could have been so mistaken. So totally ignorant of the ways of pleasing a man. And she had only herself to blame.

'No,' he said hoarsely. 'Nothing—wrong.' He pronounced the word as if he'd never heard it before.

Slowly he altered his position, lowering himself towards her, his gaze intent, so that he was easily within her reach. Close enough for her to go on touching him. If she wanted. Or if she dared…

She took a deep breath, drawing in the unique male scent of him, then began shyly, awkwardly, to stroke his face, the slant of his cheekbones, the line of his jaw, and Roan turned his head swiftly, capturing the caressing fingers with his mouth and suckling them gently and sensuously, before bending to pay the same delicious attention to her breasts, beguiling her nipples into renewed tumescence under the flicker of his tongue.

Desire pierced her again—pagan—almost violent. She made a little sound in her throat, arching towards him, and heard him groan softly in response.

'Hold me,' he commanded huskily, and Harriet obeyed, sliding her fingers up to his shoulders, only to find his own hands under her slender flanks, encouraging her to lift them and clasp them round him as he began once more to move.

Roan fastened his mouth to hers, kissing her with unrestrained and hungry passion, her response equally abandoned as they rose and sank together, locked in a stark unbridled impetus that was almost agony.

And she was lost—blind—drowning in this dark and terrifying magic, her body straining in desperate, fevered yearning for the ultimate revelation.

From some immense distance, she heard him say, 'Now…'

And suddenly it was there—the fierce shuddering frenzy of pleasure—incredibly raw—wildly intensified. And she was soaring—crying out, her voice unrecognisable, as the harsh miracle of rapture consumed her, drained her, and flung her back, mindless and exhausted, to this room, this bed—and this man.

Leaving her trembling and sated under his weight, their damp flesh clinging, their bodies still united, his head heavy against her breasts in the wake of his own hoarsely groaned fulfilment. And feeling the glory of a triumph all her own.

CHAPTER SEVEN

SHE should move, Harriet thought drowsily—eventually. She should be pushing him away and telling him to go—now that he'd had what he wanted. Yet—somehow—she wanted to stay exactly where she was, enjoying those last fading echoes of blissful satisfaction. Maybe even—sleep.

Only to realise that Roan was the one on the move—lifting himself away from her, and swinging his legs to the floor. He stood up, stretching lazily, then sauntered across to the bathroom.

Not a look—not a word in her direction, thought Harriet, turning on to her side, and reaching down to pull the sheet defensively over her body. Forbidding herself to watch him go.

She heard the sound of the lavatory flushing, then, a moment later, the rush of water from her high-powered shower.

My God, she thought, stoking her resentment, he's behaving as if he belongs here. As if we'd been married for ever.

On the other hand, while he was occupied with washing himself, it meant that she was alone with her clothes—her bag—her key within reach, and if she was very quick, and very quiet, she could be dressed and gone before he knew it.

But where? There were plenty of hotels, but they might take a dim view of someone arriving in the middle of the night without a reservation or proper luggage. Or she could always go to Tessa and Bill, but that was bound to involve the kind of awkward explanations she was anxious to avoid.

Anyway, if she was honest, wasn't it altogether too late for flight? A case of locking the stable door long after the horse's departure?

And wouldn't it also send Roan all the wrong messages, implying that she was scared? When what she needed to do was convince him that nothing that had happened between them made the slightest difference to her. That he didn't feature, even marginally, in her general scheme of things.

That he never had, and he never would.

However, she might also need to convince herself, she thought with a sudden thud of the heart, her teeth grazing the swollen fullness of her lower lip. And what kind of admission was that?

Oh, God, she thought, what a hideous mess I've made of everything.

When Roan came back into the bedroom, he was wearing a towel draped round his hips, and using another to dry his hair. A faint aroma of her favourite carnation soap accompanied him.

She said glacially, 'Don't hesitate to make yourself quite at home.'

'Thank you, *agapi mou*.' His tone held faint amusement as he glanced round him. 'But, somehow, I don't think it will ever be that.' He paused. 'I have run a bath for you.'

She stared up at him. 'Why?'

Roan shrugged. 'You did not join me in the shower, as I had hoped, and I thought you might appreciate it—after your exertions.' He slanted a smile at her. 'Warm water is soothing—for the temper as well as the body, Harriet *mou*. But the choice is yours.'

'It's a little late for that,' she said, ignoring his reference to the shower. 'As you made sure.'

'Not all the time—if you remember.' The dark eyes challenged her to argue, knowing, of course, that she couldn't do so—damn him. 'Don't let the water get cold,' he added softly, and wandered into the living room.

Harriet sent a furious look after him, but couldn't think of a single reason not to take his advice. She eased herself out from the concealing sheet, keeping a wary eye open for his possible return, and almost scampered into the bathroom.

Not just water waiting for her either, she realised, as she sank, sighing, through the thick layer of scented bubbles produced by her most expensive bath oil, and rested her head against the little quilted pillow fixed to the back of the tub.

She wasn't accustomed to such pampering, and it annoyed her, because it was soporific too. And she needed to think—and fast— what to do next. How she could possibly face him in view of the appalling weakness she'd displayed—what she could say in her own defence. But for the moment it was easier simply to drift...

'Will you drink some champagne with me?'

Her eyes flew open, and she sat up with a start, aware with vexation that she hadn't heard his approach. She wrapped an arm across her breasts, watching with hostility as he sat down on the rim of the tub, holding out one of the flutes of pale, sparkling wine he was carrying.

'Where did this come from?' She knew there was none in the flat.

'I brought it,' he said, adding softly, 'I regret it is not properly chilled, but perhaps you could glare at it.'

She scowled at him instead. 'You think we actually have something to celebrate?' she asked scornfully.

'Why, yes,' he said. 'I do.' He looked pointedly down at his shoulder, and she saw, mortified, that her nails had left faint red marks on the smooth skin. 'Now, take your wine.' He observed her reluctant compliance with amusement. 'What shall we drink to? The future, perhaps?'

'To going our separate ways,' Harriet said curtly. 'That's the only aspect of the future that appeals to me.'

'In spite of all that we have just been to each other?' Roan asked mockingly. 'You grieve me. But let it be as you wish.' He touched his glass to hers, and drank, and she unwillingly followed suit, feeling the wine burst like sunlight in her dry mouth. A good vintage, she thought, surprised, and deserving of a better occasion.

'Thank you.' With a defiant flourish, she tipped the rest of the wine into the water, and handed him the empty glass. 'I presume you have no other toasts to propose.'

'I can think of none that would be appropriate.' His voice was quiet.

'So, perhaps now this—ritual humiliation is complete, you'll go, and leave me in peace.'

'I came here to spend the night, Harriet *mou*. And it is not over yet.'

'But you—got what you wanted.' She stumbled over the words. 'Why are you doing this?'

'And why are you so ashamed of being a woman?'

It wasn't the reply Harriet had expected, and she lifted her chin. 'I'm not. It's the shame of letting myself become involved with you that I can't handle. I should have realised that, with you, poor doesn't necessarily mean honest. That you're just a manipulative, womanising swine, and I don't know how I'm going to live with myself after—after what you've done to me.'

There was a brief tingling silence, then he said quietly, 'Then I have nothing to lose.' He drank the rest of his wine, set both glasses down, and stood up.

Before she knew what was happening, his hands were under her armpits, lifting her bodily out of the water. He reached for one of the bath sheets on the warm rail, and enveloped her in it, muffling her indignant protest.

'Dry yourself,' he instructed curtly. 'Then come back to bed. It is time your sexual education was resumed.'

Her heart was pounding unevenly. She said chokingly, 'You mean you're determined to find other ways to degrade me.'

His smile was jeering. 'Why, yes, my innocent. Believe me, the possibilities are endless, and I look forward to exploring them with you.' He unfastened the towel he was wearing and casually dropped it into the linen basket. 'So, do not keep me waiting too long,' he added, as he left her.

Slowly, Harriet blotted the moisture from her skin, staring at herself in the mirror, trying to recognise the girl who'd swung out of the flat that morning on her way to finalise a simple business arrangement. Who'd believed the situation was under her control, and that she'd emerge a winner. And that she was—untouchable.

Well, she knew better now. The image looking back at her had eyes the colour of smoke, and the outline of her mouth was blurred from kissing.

This is not me, she thought. He's turned me into someone I don't know, and never wanted to be. And crazily, impossibly, I—let it happen. But how—and why? He called this our wedding night, but it could never be that. Because he's the last person wanting to be a husband, and I have no intention of being a wife.

So, it's just a one-night stand. Payback time because I made him look foolish in front of witnesses. After all, he pretty much admitted it.

And, if not for revenge, why else would he want—this? Me?

She dropped the damp towel, and studied her nude reflection dispassionately. It couldn't be for her looks—or her figure. She was moderately attractive, no more, and reed-slender. And it certainly wasn't for the sweetness of her disposition, she told herself wryly.

She supposed a virgin in her mid-twenties had a certain novelty value in twenty-first-century London, but why would he bother when there were so many more exciting—and willing—women around?

Except she had been—willing. Eventually. And that was the open wound she would take with her from this encounter. The bitter knowledge that she hadn't fought tooth and nail against the ultimate surrender. That the marks she'd inflicted on his body were the result of passion, not self-defence.

She hadn't even managed the frozen submission she'd planned as her last line of retreat. And now it was much too late.

She took a last glance at herself, and turned away, knowing that she couldn't simply walk back naked into the bedroom. Without mental or emotional connection between them, his dark scrutiny would be a stinging embarrassment, she thought, as she trod over to the fitted unit beside the basin, and opened the bottom drawer.

The neatly folded cotton housecoat that lay there was quite the oldest garment she possessed. High-necked and demure, it had been at school with her, and its pattern of tiny rosebuds had almost faded away with repeated launderings over the years. Hanging on to it was sheer sentiment, but it had the virtue of being opaque—a veil for her to hide behind as she went to him.

He was lying on his back, arms folded behind his head, staring up at the ceiling as she walked towards the bed, and she noticed that he'd tidied the pillows, and drawn the sheet up to waist level. He turned to look at her, and she saw his eyes widen, and braced herself for some numbing piece of sarcasm.

But when he spoke his voice was almost reflective. 'So now I know how you looked when you were a little girl, Harriet *mou*.'

She gave him a quick, startled glance, then turned her back while she removed the soft folds, then slid under the covering sheet. And waited, nerves jangling, for him to reach for her.

'Expecting another seduction, *matia mou*?' He broke the silence at last, just as her inner tension was nearing screaming point. 'Because it is not going to happen.' And as she twisted round to stare at him he added, 'This time, I wish you to make love to me.'

'*Oh, God, no—no...*'

She only realised she'd spoken the thought aloud when she saw his mouth twist in a wry smile.

He shook his head. 'Why, Harriet?' He made her name sound like a caress. 'Don't you like being in bed with me—just a little?'

There was no need to answer. And no point in trying to lie either. The sudden blaze of colour warming her face was betrayal enough. And the helpless clench of desire deep inside her.

'I enjoyed having you touch me,' he went on softly. 'It's a pleasure I wish to be repeated. And you seemed to like it too, my shy bride, so why don't you come much—much closer, and kiss me?'

She obeyed slowly, helplessly, moving across the space that divided them, until she felt the warmth of him against her, and the tingling thrill of response in her own skin.

She swallowed, her heart thudding, then leaned over him, her hair spilling around him in a fragrant cloud, as she let the rosy peaks of her breasts brush his chest, deliberately tantalising the flat male nipples. She heard him catch his breath.

He said huskily, 'Harriet, my sweet one—*agapi mou*.'

And she paused, her mouth a fraction from his.

'But I don't love you,' she whispered fiercely back to him. 'And I never will.'

Harriet awoke slowly, pushing herself up through the layers of sleep like a swimmer surfacing from the dark depths of a timeless sea, and finding sunlight. She waited for the usual stress to kick in, but it was strangely absent. Instead, she felt totally relaxed, her whole body toned—suffused with unaccustomed well-being.

Realising, as she forced open her weighted eyelids, that she was actually smiling.

And then she remembered…

She shot upright, gasping, clutching the sheet to her breasts, staring dazedly down at the empty bed beside her, heart hammering. Wondering for an instant if her imagination had been playing tricks on her—if she'd simply dreamt it—all of it.

But the voluptuous tenderness between her thighs soon disabused her of that notion. She had to face the fact that she'd spent most of the previous night having sex, with an increasing hunger and lack of inhibition that made her quail as she recalled it now in daylight.

Unable, it seemed, to get enough of him, she thought, turning over to bury her burning face in her pillow. Or to give enough either…

I wish you to make love to me.

And she'd done so, following instincts she barely understood, hesitant, even gauche at first, but learning quickly, guided by Roan's glance, his whispered word, even an indrawn breath. Discovering intimacies she could never have imagined she'd permit, let alone enjoy.

Until, at the last, she'd found herself astride him, absorbing him with exquisite totality, her body bent in an arc of pleasure as she pursued, with him, yet another release that was as savage as it was mutual.

They'd finally fallen asleep from sheer exhaustion, still entwined. Harriet could remember waking around dawn, and finding she was sprawled across him, imprisoned by his arm, her cheek pressed against the heavy beat of his heart. And when she'd tried gingerly to move to a more decorous distance, Roan had muttered something sleepily in his own language, his grasp tightening around her. So she'd stayed, and slept again.

Yet he'd had no problem extricating himself, it seemed. And she'd been too dead to the world to notice. Had expected to find him there, holding her, when she woke. Had wanted him to be there…

Now, there was an admission.

She sat up again, pushing back her tumble of hair, listening for the sound of the shower, trying to detect a hint of coffee in the air—

any indication that he was still around. Somewhere. But there was only silence, and the sunlight pressing against the blinds far more brightly than it should have done.

Biting her lip, Harriet glanced at the bedside clock and stifled a yelp. He'd gone, and so had half the morning, which meant that for the first time she was going to be horrifyingly late for work.

She stood under the shower, letting the water stream over her body, touching every part of her that his hands—his mouth—had caressed. Rinsing away the carnation-scented lather, remembering its fragrance on his skin, and now she'd breathed it—licked at it. Remembering altogether too much, she thought breathlessly, bracing a hand against the tiled wall for support because her legs were shaking under her again. And these memories had to be dealt with— barred—if she was ever to know any peace again.

As she went to discard her used towel in the linen basket, she saw a glimmer of peach satin, and realised he'd collected her pyjamas from the floor, as if he knew she only wore things once before laundering. Although, in this case, she'd hardly had the chance to wear them at all.

She hunted discontentedly along the rail in her wardrobe, wishing there was something else to choose apart from black, black and yet more black. 'Those shapeless garments,' he'd called them, and much good they'd done her.

Now there seemed little point in persevering with her camouflage, and it would have been nice to wear something light and bright—something that floated—on this glorious sunlit morning.

Then paused, her lips twisting in self-derision. 'And what does that make you, my dear?' she wondered aloud. 'A butterfly emerging from its chrysalis, or the same dreary moth with delusions? Get back to square one where you belong.'

It occurred to her, as she scraped her hair back into its usual style, that she was ravenous. No point in being late on an empty stomach, she thought, as she dashed into her smart galley kitchen, slipping bread into the toaster, and switching on the kettle.

There was no sign of Roan having breakfasted. Not so much as a cup of coffee, she noticed, but perhaps he felt he'd helped himself to quite enough already. And if that was intended as a joke, it hadn't worked, she told herself with a pang.

She ladled honey on to her toast, eating and drinking standing up, before grabbing her bag and racing to the door.

At first sight, the living room was in its usual pristine condition, with no trace of him there either. And then she saw the piece of paper lying on her ash table, a sheet torn at random, it seemed, from a sketch block, the edges ragged. And in the middle of it, a small circle of gold.

The wedding ring, she thought, that she'd handed back to him yesterday with such insouciance. And scrawled across the paper in thick black letters the single word, 'Souvenir.'

So it had been revenge, she thought, feeling suddenly numb. Amongst all the disastrous mistakes she'd made last night, she'd been right about that, at least.

I couldn't have made it easier for him if I'd tried, she thought. Or sweeter.

And somehow I have to learn to live with that.

By the time Harriet reached the office, the weekly round-up meeting had already begun.

'Nice of you to join us, Miss Flint,' Tony commented acidly.

'I'm sorry.' Harriet sat down, needled by the sight of Jon Audley exchanging complicit grins with Anthea. 'My alarm didn't go off.' *Largely because I forgot to set it, having so many other things to think about at the time. Most of which I don't want to contemplate.*

And her inner turmoil had been further compounded by an encounter with George, the concierge, as he sorted the mail in the foyer. His beaming smile, and the faint archness of his, 'Good morning, Mrs Zandros,' had totally stymied any rebuke she'd been considering over the matter of the key, and she'd simply mumbled a flushed response and fled.

'How brave of it,' said Tony, recalling her sharply to the here and now. 'How did things go yesterday, by the way?'

For a moment she stared at him, totally thrown once again. 'What do you mean?' Her voice was a croak.

'At Hayford House.' He held out his hand. 'I presume you've already written up your report with your usual blazing efficiency.'

She took a deep steadying breath. *Think!* 'Actually, no,' she returned calmly. 'As nothing has changed diametrically since the last report was produced, I thought it would be simpler to work from that.' She looked at Jonathan. 'I presume you still have a copy on file.'

There was a silence, then he said curtly, 'I didn't write one. I simply got on to our maintenance people and—requested a visit.'

'And made a follow-up call to ensure it had been carried out?'

'I didn't suppose it was necessary.' Jon's look spoke daggers. 'They're pretty reliable, and God knows there weren't any major issues.'

'No,' Harriet said reflectively. 'And the tenants appreciated how busy you are.' She allowed another awkward silence to establish itself, then glanced back at Tony's annoyed face. 'I'll get on to it as soon as the meeting is over.' *But will that be before or after I call Isobel…?*

At any other time she'd have been jubilant having scored a minor triumph over the obnoxious Audley, but, set against everything else going on in her life, it barely registered, and she was aware she was frankly sleep-walking her way through the rest of the meeting.

And the remainder of the morning wasn't much better. Her concentration was shot to pieces, her thinking dominated by the memory of last night, and her need to make sense of what had happened. And, of course, deal with it.

Three times she reached for the phone and began to dial Isobel's number. Three times she got halfway, only to abandon the call.

I can't talk to her yet, she thought. I'm too confused. Besides, what on earth can I say? Tell her I want an injunction against him, followed by the quickest divorce in the history of the world? How many awkward explanations will that throw up?

'What's the matter? Have a bad night?'

She jumped almost convulsively as she looked up to see Tony watching her from the doorway.

Colour stormed into her face. 'No,' she returned defensively. 'Why do you ask?'

He frowned. 'Because you've been looking white as a ghost—

totally wiped out. Just as if...' He paused, looking faintly embarrassed. 'Well, that doesn't matter.'

He strolled forward, hands in pockets. 'Yet now you could be running a temperature,' he commented critically. 'Sure you're all right? Not sickening for something?'

She stared at the screen in front of her. 'I don't think so.'

'Good.' He hesitated again, then said almost gently, 'You know, Harriet, you don't have to drive yourself so hard all the time. Maybe you should take some time off—chill out a little. No one would think less of you.'

Her voice was quiet. 'I might.' *Because the job I do is—me. I can't let go of that. I dare not.*

'That's what I'm trying to get at.' Tony sighed. 'Being Gregory Flint's granddaughter does not require you to be one hundred per cent perfect. You're allowed to make mistakes.'

She didn't look at him. 'Even though mistakes can be dangerous?' *And when I've just made one—a terrible one—bordering on total disaster. A mistake which is making me wonder about myself—ask questions I don't want to answer?*

'Even then,' he said. 'It could perhaps ease things round here as well. Improve office relationships.'

She drew a swift breath. 'To do a sloppy job?'

'No,' he said. 'To be human. Maybe that missed alarm was a signal.' He paused. 'Look—take the rest of the day off. Shop—take a walk in the park—go home and catch up on your sleep. Anything that will relax you. And it's not a suggestion, Harriet,' he added briskly, seeing she was about to protest. 'I'm telling you to do it.'

At the doorway, he paused. 'Oh, and leave the laptop. That's another order.'

Harriet stared after him. Wasn't there one department of her life where she was still allowed a choice? she asked herself in a kind of desperation.

She had a curious feeling that the foundations on which she'd constructed her existence were being eroded, and the entire structure was beginning to totter.

And it was humiliating being sent home like this—like an unruly pupil being made to stand in a school corridor, she thought stormily, as she grabbed her bag and made for the lift, glad there was no one around to witness her departure.

But once outside the building, she stood irresolute, a little lost without the usual pattern of the day to rely on. Shopping had no attraction whatsoever, a solitary walk would only start her thinking all over again, and the prospect of an early return to the flat was even more unappealing.

Because, thanks to Roan, it was no longer her refuge—her private sanctuary. And last night's memories were still too potent.

Mrs Zandros, she thought, sinking her teeth into the tenderness of her lower lip. *Mrs Zandros*.

She straightened her shoulders, telling herself that the hollow feeling inside her was probably due to hunger. She'd made use of the lunchtime sandwich service, but only eaten half of her ham and salad order, and knew there was still nothing waiting in the refrigerator.

And planning her evening meal would be an occupation of sorts.

There was a good delicatessen not far away and, after some deliberation, she picked a cheese and spinach tart, with a selection of salads, and some ciabatta bread, then added a carton of strawberries and one of nectarines to her haul. In a neighbouring off-licence, she selected a bottle of her favourite Chablis, and found herself pausing at the flower stall on her way to the Tube to buy a mass of freesias.

I must be mad, she thought blankly, as she sat on the train inhaling their scent. I don't even have a vase.

Back at the flat, she unpacked the food, and put it in the fridge with the wine. The freesias she divided between three of the tall, elegant, designer goblets she normally used for mineral water, and placed them round the room.

Then she rolled up her sleeves and set to work, starting in the bedroom. She stripped the bed completely, and remade it with fresh linen, then turned her attention to the bathroom. Freeing herself of the taint of last night, she thought, wishing she could scrub him from her mind as easily. And that she could rid herself of the *ache* of him in her newly awakened flesh.

I despise myself.

But it was no use to think like that. She had to pull herself together, and put the memory of him away with her wedding ring, which she placed in the box containing the pearls Gramps had given her when she was eighteen, and pushed to the back of a drawer.

When she had showered and changed into a pair of aquamarine pyjamas—the peach ones and her robe she'd bundled into a plastic sack to bury in her rubbish bin—she sat down to eat. She found she was glancing round, looking at the flat as if through a stranger's eyes. She supposed it was—a little sparse, as if she was just passing through rather than making her home there. But then Gracemead was her real home, and always would be, so why would she need another?

She'd never thought of asking Gramps if she could bring anything from the house to London. There was a pretty desk in the morning room, she thought, and a rocking chair in what had been the nursery. Perhaps she'd mention them next time she went down.

Elsewhere, she might replace the blinds with curtains. Look for a rug. Some cushions, possibly.

She might even stop living out of freezer cabinets and delis. Buy some real food, and learn to cook it herself on that almost-new stove. And she could even ask Mrs Wade to write out some of her favourite recipes, although she'd better make sure the good woman was sitting down first, she thought wryly.

She cleared away, and came back into the living room. The silence in the flat was beginning to feel faintly oppressive. But she'd always been fine on her own in the past, and would be again. This—edginess was just a temporary thing.

However, it would have been good to travel down to Gracemead tomorrow, she thought wistfully. But that was impossible, as she could hardly show up, a bride of two days, without her husband.

In a few weeks' time, it would be different. She could find excuses for his absence, and pretend she was dashing back eagerly to be reunited with him, she told herself, stiffening against the renewed pain that slashed at her.

She could do—whatever she had to.

And when Gracemead finally belonged to her, it would all seem worthwhile. Her temporary marriage little more than a bad dream. The telephone rang and she jumped, hurrying over to answer it. 'Tessa.' Her voice lilted. 'How lovely. When did you get back? Oh, I'm fine— same as ever, you know. Lunch on Sunday? That would be great.'

Something really to look forward to, she thought, as she replaced the receiver, and tried to forget that just for a moment, when she'd heard her friend's voice, she'd felt a sharp stab of disappointment.

CHAPTER EIGHT

'ARE you really all right?' said Tessa.

Harriet met her scrutiny with an assumption of calmness. 'Don't I look it?'

'No, frankly you look—peaky. More so than when we went away.'

'Then it's as well I brought a tonic.' Harriet deposited the bottle of champagne she'd brought on the kitchen table. 'You, of course, look amazing,' she added, admiring her friend's delicate golden tan displayed in a strapless top and brief shorts. 'And I'm probably just starving. What's that heavenly smell?'

Tessa shrugged. 'Roast beef and the usual trimmings,' she returned wryly. 'It's too hot for that, really, but Bill put in a special request, and, as you know, I can deny him nothing.'

She jerked a thumb towards the glass doors which stood open on to the patio, and the sound of distant and muffled cursing. 'He's putting up a bird table.'

She lifted her voice mellifluously. 'Leave that, darling. Harriet's here, and she's brought fizz.'

Her husband joined them, sucking his knuckles. 'Damn all birds.' He dropped a kiss on his wife's hair on his way to open the wine. 'Everything all right, Harry, love?' His glance was questioning. 'You look…'

'Peaky,' Tessa supplied helpfully as he hesitated.

'Well, certainly in need of a break.' He poured the champagne, and handed round the glasses. 'You ought to try Greece, sweetheart. Great place to unwind.'

Harriet smiled brightly. 'I'll have to take your word for that.' *Because it's the last place on earth I'd ever choose.*

'All the same,' Tessa said, 'it's good to be back.'

'So, what's new with you, Harry?' Bill asked, leaning back in his chair. 'How's the on-going battle with your grandfather? Persuaded him to see reason yet?'

You don't want to know what I've done, thought Harriet, studying the rising bubbles in her glass. Aloud, she said, 'Let's say that I— live in hope.'

Bill downed his champagne and stood up. 'And I'd better get back to my hammering.' He looked at Harriet. 'Care to lose a thumb in a good cause?'

'Love to,' Harriet murmured. 'But I'm actually going to stay here, and watch your wife perform her magic. See if I can pick up a few tips for the future.'

Tessa's eyes gleamed. 'You're planning to start cooking? My God, are you telling us that at last you've met someone?'

For a moment, Harriet was seriously jolted. *They don't know— they can't know…* Somehow she managed a tone of surprised amusement. 'Whatever do you mean?'

'Well,' Tessa said, 'apparently, when *the man* comes into your life, the first thing you want to do is feed him. Which was certainly true in our case. I couldn't wait to impress Bill with my culinary skills.' She paused, looking across at her husband and smiling, her face suddenly dreamy. 'And the second thing, it seems, is to have his baby.'

'Oh.' Harriet stared at them both, beginning to smile too. 'Does this mean…?'

'It certainly does,' said Bill. 'Harry—you're going to be a godmother.'

'Oh.' Harriet took a deep breath. 'But that's—just wonderful,' she said huskily. 'I'm so happy for you both. When did you find out?'

'It was confirmed just before we went away. So we had the whole two weeks to talk about it, and make plans.' Tessa paused. 'For starters, I'm handing in my notice at work.'

'But you love your job.'

'They've been good years,' her friend agreed. 'But now I have other priorities. And I'm tired of racing the other rats.' She sighed. 'Love, I'm sure you won't approve, or understand, but I feel it's right for me, so please try.'

'You mean from my position as hard-faced career bitch?' Harriet went round the table and hugged them both fiercely. 'Sorry, guys, but I think it's a great decision.'

'Oh, babe.' Tessa gulped mistily. 'I wish I could see you as happy.'

'I will be,' Harriet promised. 'Just not in the same way, that's all.'

It was a marvellous lunch, a celebration full of sunshine and laughter, with delicious food, from the chilled cucumber soup, through the perfectly cooked beef, and down to the summer pudding with clotted cream.

Harriet found she was watching the pair of them in a whole new way, her consciousness heightened as she saw how they interacted with each other, the way they looked and spoke. The small private smiles—the tender awareness.

Real people, she thought, swallowing past a painful lump in her throat, in a real marriage. And a million miles from the doomed pretence that I've brought on myself.

She was assailed by a sudden vivid memory of the strong beat of Roan's heart under her cheek—the way he'd drawn her closer, when, in truth, she hadn't wanted to escape at all. Falling asleep feeling so safe—so strangely secure in his arms.

Then waking to find it was an illusion.

I want what you two have, she thought, pain twisting inside her. But something tells me I'm never going to be that lucky.

It was late in the afternoon when she finally tore herself away, promising that they'd all meet up again very soon.

But, sitting huddled in the back of the cab, she felt the joy of the day fading to be replaced by an overwhelming bleakness, and knew suddenly but very surely that she didn't want to go back to the isolation of the flat.

That she had a very different destination in mind.

Abruptly, she leaned forward and directed the driver to take her to Hildon Yard.

Just to see him again, she told herself. That's all. To sit down and talk—properly for once. Maybe attempt to work out if anything can be salvaged from this—non-marriage. Not living together, of course, she added hastily, but—seeing each other sometimes. As friends and—perhaps, occasional lovers.

If that's possible. I—I don't seem to know any more. Can't figure what's happening to me.

On the other hand, she could always abandon the subtle approach altogether, and throw herself at him, ripping his clothes off as she did so.

A third possibility was that he might not be there at all, and she would have to leave another message on his mobile phone, and hope that he picked it up. Arrange another meeting on neutral territory, to try and reach some understanding.

There was also a chance that he might not want to see her—or he might laugh when he learned why she'd come to him.

But to spend the rest of her life wondering if things could have been different would be far worse.

Even though it was Sunday afternoon, the yard was busy, and Harriet skirted gingerly round its edge, grimacing at the noise from the wagons as they were being loaded.

She stopped to allow one to reverse, pressing herself against the wall. As she waited, she realised that the door to the studio had opened, and Roan was walking out on to the staircase. But not alone.

She saw the gleam of his companion's blonde hair in the late afternoon sunlight, as they stood talking, heads bent. Watched as the girl put up a hand and touched his cheek, and he took her in his arms and held her.

Harriet stood, transfixed. She thought stupidly, But it's the weekend, and she's married. Where does her husband think she is? Or doesn't she care? And then, more cogently, Oh, God, I've got to get out of here—now. Before I'm seen.

She retreated slowly back the way she'd come, telling herself she should be thankful that she hadn't arrived earlier. That she hadn't barged in and—found them together. At least she'd been saved that particular humiliation. But not the agony of her own imaginings.

When she got outside, her taxi was just drawing away, and she

chased after it, waving and calling to the driver. Then saw with
relief the brake lights come on.

'Something wrong, love?' The man peered curiously at her as she
appeared beside him.

'No.' Harriet spoke breathlessly, stumbling over the words. 'I've
changed my mind, that's all.' She paused, before adding in a voice
she didn't recognise, 'Just—changed my mind.'

CHAPTER NINE

HARRIET stared at the telephone she was holding as if it had turned into a black mamba.

She said, articulating the words with immense care, 'Gramps—you—are coming to the exhibition at the Parsifal?'

'Naturally,' Gregory Flint returned with a touch of impatience. 'Surely Roan told you I'd been invited?'

No, she wanted to scream. Roan has told me nothing, because I've had no contact with him since our… Since we…

And when my own invitation arrived, I tore it into very small pieces and binned them. Not that he'd sent it, of course.

She said almost pleadingly, 'But you hate London.'

'As a general rule,' her grandfather agreed. 'But this is something of a special occasion. The evening when we all discover if your faith in your husband's artistic prowess is justified. You must be nervous.'

I wasn't, she thought grimly, until I took this call.

'Besides,' he went on more genially, 'I want to see how married life agrees with you both. It's important to me, as I'm sure you realise.'

In other words, she was not out of the wood yet, Harriet thought, her stomach beginning to churn. Because she was being warned that he expected to see a display of marital harmony along with the paintings. Which under the circumstances was a sick joke—and she wasn't laughing.

She said woodenly, 'Yes, of course. And it's a lovely surprise.'

She paused. 'And I'd be delighted to dine at your club. Shall we say six-thirty?'

'I look forward to it, my dear,' he said, and rang off.

Oh, God, Harriet thought, sinking limply on to the sofa. What the hell do I do now? Another lousy day at work, and now this.

But there was only one genuine course of action open to her, and she knew it. She would have to talk to Roan, however painful that promised to be. Have to come to some accommodation with him, or her plans for Gracemead—and her entire future with it—would collapse in ruins.

I'll do it now, she thought. Before I have a chance to think what I'm doing, and talk myself out of it. Besides, Roan can hardly refuse to co-operate as it's entirely his fault that Grandfather's coming to London.

But would he see it that way?

It was irritating beyond reason to realise that he seemed to have ignored her strictures to avoid all contact with Gregory Flint. On the other hand, who was to say who'd made the first approach? Two men, she thought broodingly, with wills of their own.

The studio door was shut as she walked up the iron staircase.

She knocked loudly, and waited. If Roan was with his mistress, it would at least give them a chance to get their clothes on, she thought stonily, resisting the inevitable stab of anguish. But the door opened without any hasty scuffling, and Roan confronted her, barefoot, but otherwise fully clad in the usual shabby jeans, and an elderly blue shirt. For a moment, he stared at her, his face without expression.

Then he said slowly, an odd note in his voice, 'Harriet—it's you. What are you doing here?'

'I'm sorry if it's an inconvenient time, but I need—to talk to you.' How was it possible to speak when her mouth was so dry? 'If—if that's all right.'

'Of course.' He gave a slight shake of the head. 'I—did not expect… But no matter,' he added more briskly. 'Come in.'

'Oh.' As she entered, she checked, looking round her. 'Nearly all the paintings have gone.'

'They have been disappearing at intervals over the past week,' he said, drily. 'But you, of course, would not know that.'

'Yet you still have the angry painting.' She walked across and looked at it. 'The one that was hanging in Luigi's restaurant. I thought it was sold.'

'It is. The owner collects it tomorrow morning.' He came to stand beside her. 'You think it shows anger? You are perceptive.'

She was deeply conscious of how near he was to her. But reluctant to betray it by moving away.

'That's a pretty sandal,' she commented, trying to sound casual. 'Expensive too. The owner must have been sorry to lose it.'

'I think she had other issues to concern her at the time.' There was a cynical note in his voice. 'Not that it matters any longer.'

He sent her a level look. 'But I am sure you did not come here to discuss my work, or its motivation.' He paused. 'Would you like to sit down? May I offer you some coffee—a glass of wine?'

'No, thank you,' she returned crisply, turning away. Putting space between them. 'This isn't a social call.' But he could well be expecting company, she thought, swallowing. One quick, all-encompassing glance had shown her that the clutter and mess from her previous visit had been removed along with the pictures. The place looked clean and tidy, and the screened-off bed appeared to be made up with fresh white linen. But perhaps that was a refinement insisted on by his most frequent visitor, she thought with a pang.

'And I prefer to stand,' she added, ignoring the sofa with its invitingly plumped cushions.

'As you wish.' He watched her, hands on hips, the black linen skirt and tunic that was her working gear dismissed in one derisive glance, which turned to a frown as he noted her bare left hand. 'So, what is the problem, Harriet *mou*? Have I contravened some other precious, unwritten code?'

'Pretty much,' she said shortly. 'I discovered a short time ago that my grandfather is coming to the opening of your show at the gallery. And that he expects to see us there—together. As if we were really married.'

'But we are really married, *yineka mou*.' His tone was harsh. 'Even if you still refuse to wear my ring. Do you wish me to—jog your memory, perhaps?'

For a moment, she felt her body quiver in sheer yearning. Knew that if he drew her down on to the floorboards, she would welcome him into her. Would take as completely as she gave.

But it wasn't going to happen. She had to fight this devastating weakness, she thought, lifting her chin defiantly. 'I'd really prefer you to disappear from my life altogether, but you've made that impossible.'

'Not necessarily,' he said. 'I am planning to return to Greece. Will that put sufficient distance between us, or do you wish me to consider possibilities in Australia?' His voice bit.

Greece? For a moment, Harriet felt dizzy. He was leaving, she thought. Going away. And if he did, it was probable she would never see him again, and he must not—*must not*—see that it might matter.

She said coldly, 'Just now, my primary consideration is how we're going to get through the next twenty four hours without blowing our deal sky-high.' She drew a deep breath. 'I wasn't actually planning to attend the opening, but now it seems I must.'

She ignored whatever it was he'd muttered under his breath in his own language, and went resolutely on. 'I must also pretend that you and I have—a relationship. But I can't do it alone. I need you to—back me up.'

'Why, Harriet *mou*,' Roan said mockingly, 'have you come here to ask me a favour? I am overwhelmed.'

'If you'd kept your distance from Grandfather, as I requested, it wouldn't be necessary,' Harriet said tautly.

'Don't be a fool,' he said with sudden curtness. 'And don't take him for one either. You think he would have just accepted a marriage to some mysterious husband it was never convenient for him to meet? Never.'

He paused. 'In fact, I am the one who has been trying to establish that you and I are together and happily in love, with no help from you.'

Harriet bit her lip. 'Are you saying you're prepared to—continue with the pretence—in front of my grandfather. That you'll help me?'

He shrugged. 'Why not? It's only one evening. But you have to play your part too.' His dark gaze met hers. Held it as he spoke briskly. 'Don't flinch if I touch you. When I kiss you, offer me your lips, and don't be too ready to break away. Remember that we are lovers, newly married, who know what pleasure their bodies can share, and who cannot wait to be alone.

'And no black shrouds,' he added harshly. 'Wear a dress—something that makes you look like a woman. A woman who expects—and wants—to be undressed later in the evening. Understand?'

Yes, she thought, her throat tightening. Oh, yes, she understood. She didn't look at him. 'I—don't have anything like that.'

'Then buy it.' His tone was clipped. 'After all, it's a big night for me, *pedhi mou*, and my wife will be expected to do me credit, so wear some make-up too. Paint your nails, and put my ring on your hand as if it belonged there.'

He looked her over again. 'And wear your hair loose.'

She said in a stifled voice, 'Very well, if those are your terms. Then I'll see you when I bring my grandfather to the gallery tomorrow.'

'Leaving so soon?' His brows lifted. 'I am desolate.'

'Don't worry,' she said. 'I'm sure you'll soon find solace.'

'Are you, Harriet *mou*? I wish I could be so sure.' Roan moved his shoulders indolently, almost wearily under the thin blue cotton shirt, then began slowly to unbutton it, still watching her.

'What—what do you think you're doing?' She was ashamed of the quiver in her tone, as she recalled the last time she'd seen him do this. And its aftermath.

'Exactly what I intended before your arrival,' he returned casually. 'I have had a tough day, finishing an important commission. So, I plan a hot shower, followed by—relaxation of some kind.' He took off the shirt. Dropped it to the floor beside him.

'Then I'll leave you to it.' Harriet turned away too hastily, aware that he was behind her, following her to the door.

He said softly, 'Tell me something. Why did you come here tonight when it would have been simpler to telephone?'

'As you said, I wanted a favour, and I wasn't sure you'd agree.' She reached for the door handle. 'It—it seemed more polite to ask in person. Argue my case, if I had to.'

'And was that your only reason?' His hand closed over hers.

'Yes,' she said hoarsely. 'Of course. And I—have to go.'

'Without what you really came for?' He was stroking her fingers, his breath warm, stirring the fine hairs on the nape of her neck. His voice held a quiet urgency. 'Why deny what we both know? That if you stayed with me tonight, *agapi mou*, we'd have no need of pretence tomorrow.'

Oh, God, she thought, swallowing. Was she really so transparent? The hunger he'd awoken in her so hideously, shamingly obvious? It seemed so.

All she would have to do was turn, and she would be in his arms. The arms she'd watched closing around another girl. Holding her near. Which she must never forget.

She wrenched her hand free. 'With you, it would always be pretence.' Her voice was a knife. 'You rate your charms rather too highly, Mr Zandros, and the sooner you go back to Greece the better. You might have more luck there. Who knows? That lady could still be looking for her shoe.'

'I am grateful for the reminder,' he said bitingly. 'Also for your opinion of me. But, in spite of your unwelcome candour, you don't have to worry. I shall not renege on tomorrow's agreement.'

He paused. 'And you should have no trouble in deceiving your grandfather, my sweet wife. Not when you lie so easily to yourself.'

He reached past her. Jerked the door open. 'Now, go,' he added with contempt.

And Harriet found herself obeying, her head bent, and her legs shaking under her. Her reason telling her she'd had a fortunate escape. Her body in mourning for its self-imposed starvation. And her emotions in chaos.

'Miss Flint—or I should really say Mrs Zandros?' Desmond Slevin came to meet her, smiling, as she walked into the Parsifal Gallery at her grandfather's side. He shook hands with the older man, at her murmured introduction, then turned back to her, raising an enquiring eyebrow. 'With your husband safely out of earshot, may I say how very lovely you look?'

She flushed a little. She'd already had to deal with Gregory Flint's surprised but wholehearted approval of her appearance, yet she still wondered what Roan would think of the supple, fluid lines of her knee-length ivory silk dress, with its deeply slashed cross-over bodice, which had cost more than the rest of the items in her wardrobe put together.

Would he notice, too, that the sandals she was wearing were just as strappy and frivolous as any to be found on a Greek beach, or that, as instructed, her toes and fingers were tipped in soft coral, and her mouth painted to match? Or that her hair, conker-glossy, swung almost to her shoulders?

Also, that she was wearing no jewellery except the wedding gold on the third finger of her left hand.

Would he see how hard she had tried to please him—this last time?

'Whatever, it's still good to hear,' she said. She looked around her in amazement. 'I never expected such a crowd.'

'I did,' Desmond Slevin said with quiet satisfaction. 'And it's going really well, although it was a rush getting everything framed and hung, especially as we had to wait until the last minute for the final item. But it was worth it, even if it's another one that isn't for sale, alas.'

He paused. 'But I have a bone to pick with you, young lady. When you first came to see me, you denied any personal involvement with tonight's star. Now here you are, married to him.'

'It all happened so quickly,' Harriet excused herself, aware of Gregory Flint's interested attention. 'We met and I was—head over heels almost before I knew it.'

'Well, he's been like a cat on hot bricks, waiting for you to arrive.' Desmond Slevin signalled to a waiter, who appeared with a tray of drinks. Mr Flint accepted champagne, but Harriet took a glass of orange juice, reminding herself that she needed to keep her wits about her, and not cloud her senses with alcohol.

I've made my entrance, she thought, bracing herself. Now where's the leading man?

And felt strong arms encircle her from behind.

'*Agapi mou*. My darling.' Roan drew her back against him, nuzzling her throat. 'I thought you would never get here,' he muttered huskily. 'And you look so beautiful, I wish all these people were at the bottom of the sea.'

He relaxed his hold slightly, allowing her to breathe again. Turned to her grandfather, who was smiling his approval. 'Kyrios Flint. I am honoured.'

'And I'm delighted for you, my dear boy. I can see a lot of red stickers around the place already. It seems Harriet was quite right about your talent.'

Roan took her nerveless hand and carried it to his lips. 'I am glad to have justified her faith in me. And now there are some people I wish her to meet, if you will excuse us.'

'There's no need to go overboard with the affection,' she bit at him as he led her away. 'And who are these people, anyway?'

'There is no one—yet.' Roan's hand tightened round hers. 'But I must speak to you privately. Explain something about my life that I should have told you before our marriage. And now—tonight—it can no longer be avoided.'

An iron fist was twisting in her gut. *Blonde hair shining in the sunlight. A hand touching his cheek.* She said quickly, 'No explanations are necessary. I already know—anything I need to. And you—you're a free agent. I thought I'd made that clear.'

'No one is ever completely free. Not when others are involved. I thought I could forget that, but I have realised since that I cannot do so, and that I do not even want to. I hoped there would be more time, so I could prepare you a little, but that is no longer possible.' He drew a deep breath. 'Harriet…'

'Do forgive me, Mrs Zandros.' Desmond Slevin joined them. 'Roan, the art critic from the *Daily Tribune* would like a quick word.' He glanced from one to the other, noting the set faces. 'If that's all right.'

'It's fine.' Harriet rallied herself swiftly. Produced a smile so bright it glittered. 'I'll go on looking round, while you—wow your critic, darling.'

Roan released her hand with open reluctance. He said huskily, 'It won't take long. Wait for me here—please. We—have to talk.'

No, she thought as she turned away. That isn't it at all. What you mean is you're going to talk, and I'll have to listen. Have to hear how much in love you are. And that you've now decided to bring your affair into the open, and that's why you're returning to Greece. To keep out of the way until the fuss dies down, and you're both divorced.

But that could work to my advantage, she told herself, deliberately straightening her shoulders. Because not even Grandfather could expect me to stay married to a man who was so flagrantly unfaithful. In fact, he might give me Gracemead there and then out of·sympathy.

And I should be turning cartwheels at the prospect—so why do I feel as if I want to kneel down in the middle of all these people and howl until I have no voice left?

She stopped, staring at the nearest painting—a maelstrom of savage colour that sucked you in, and would not let you go. An assault on the senses that seemed to match the tearing confusion of emotion inside her.

'Strange, isn't it, how his work differs? Some of it's so—feral.' A couple had paused beside her, and the woman was speaking. 'And yet that portrait we just saw has an almost—lyrical quality.'

Her male companion laughed. 'Well, she's a gorgeous lady, so I expect it was painted with the eyes of love—or lust. You noticed it's not for sale? He clearly can't bear to part with it.'

They moved off, but Harriet remained where she was, as if rooted to the spot. An important commission, she thought numbly, and too personal to be sold.

She found it almost at once. Realised she'd missed it when she arrived because there'd been so many people round it.

But now she had it all to herself, in all its heart-aching beauty.

Roan had painted his lady, using little background, so that there was nothing to detract from her inherent loveliness.

She was wearing a blue silk top and trousers, her hair a shimmering mass round her face, as she sat, legs curled under her, in a corner of that battered sofa. There was a book open on her lap, but she wasn't reading. She was looking ahead of her, her eyes dreaming, full of sweet secrets.

They were joy. They were anticipation. They were love.

'Good evening, Mrs Zandros.'

The man's voice was vaguely familiar, and she turned swiftly, composing herself. 'Oh,' she said rather blankly, and then remembered. 'Mr—Maxwell, isn't it? The lawyer who witnessed the wedding.'

'Yes,' he said. He looked at the portrait. 'I may be biased, but I still reckon that's a bloody amazing piece of work.'

'It's—wonderful.' *Painted with the eyes of love...* 'But then, he's a pretty amazing painter.' Her tone was falsely bright.

'I agree.' He paused. 'Look—would you like to meet Lucy? She's just over there—see?'

Harriet saw. Tonight the girl was wearing a figure-hugging dark red dress, standing at the centre of a lively group, laughing with her companions.

Her throat tightened. 'No,' she said. 'Thank you, but I think that's going a little far even in these enlightened times.'

Jack Maxwell's face closed. 'As you wish, naturally,' he said coldly. 'I realise we didn't get off to a very good start, you and I, but things have moved on and I hoped tonight we could at least be civil.'

'Well, this is my best shot at being civilised.' She seemed to be breathing over sharpened knives. 'I—I hope Roan and Lucy will be very happy together.'

There was an odd silence, then he said slowly, 'I rather doubt that. According to my mother in law, they used to fight like cat and dog when they were kids. More like brother and sister than cousins, she said, and they still have a low boiling point now. I'm surprised the portrait got done without bloodshed.'

'Cousins?' The word emerged as a croak.

He nodded. 'Their mothers were sisters. When Vanessa came back from Greece, Roan and Lucy spent a lot of their childhood together, while his parents did the whole tug-of-love custody thing. But surely he's told you this already?'

She shook her head. 'We didn't marry to exchange confidences. You of all people should realise that.'

He looked faintly awkward. 'Well, perhaps, but I thought things might have changed a little. Anyway,' he went on, 'Roan took me to Luce's twenty-first birthday party, which is how we met. And he was best man at our wedding. We're just coming up to our third anniversary, and he offered to paint her—as a special gift for us both.' He gave her a wry look. 'You obviously saw her when she was at the studio for a sitting, and jumped to the wrong conclusion.'

She bit her lip. 'I thought they seemed—close,' she said defensively.

'They are.' He was unfazed. 'When they're not wanting to kill each other.' He grinned. 'I married into a family of great huggers.'

He paused. 'However, now you know the score, won't you come and say hello to my wife? After all, you are one of the family.'

'No,' Harriet said steadily. 'I'm not. I—I made a stupid mistake, for which I'm deeply embarrassed, but it doesn't actually alter a thing. Roan and I are not—in a marriage as such. Therefore meeting his family—friends—would be an unnecessary complication. So, you'll have to excuse me.'

She turned away almost blindly, fighting for her composure. She'd blundered badly, she thought. Been almost criminally stupid in her assumptions. But was she entirely to blame?

Because it occurred to her that Roan could have put her right about his relationship with Lucy Maxwell the day they met—if he'd wanted.

While I—I saw a molehill, and constructed a mountain. Because I was jealous. Because, from the start, I wanted him myself.

It seemed she was her mother's daughter after all, letting her body rule her brain. All for the sake of another man who was planning to leave.

To commit a far greater betrayal than any affair, and who could know that better than herself—the child who'd heard the weeping in the night?

Now, more than ever, she needed to keep him at bay. To ignore the temptation of the senses whenever he came near her, by reminding herself icily and repeatedly that their lives lay in totally different directions.

As he'd made clear. She was reaching for Gracemead. Her life—her work—centred here in England. He would be returning—where? She supposed to his father's taverna, eking out a living by painting pictures for tourists. More instant portraits turned out in minutes.

But going home—his own home in Greece—with no intention of ever coming back.

And instinct told her that if jealousy had been an agony, then loneliness would be the ultimate hell. So permitting any further intimacy between them would be inviting more pain than she could bear.

So, she would subdue the anguish in her heart, and wipe every last, precious, dangerous memory from her mind.

Let the life she'd chosen close round her once more, and keep her safe.

She took a deep unsteady breath. She couldn't stay here. She wanted—needed—to go home. But what excuse could she possibly find?

She heard Roan say her name, and realised he was walking purposefully towards her, the art critic apparently dealt with.

But nothing he had to say could have any relevance. Not any more. And, somehow, she had to make him understand that.

At the same time, she was aware of a stir running through the gallery. A man's voice was speaking, deep and imperious like her grandfather's, but with a pronounced foreign accent, clearly asking a question. And people were staring, then falling back, as if clearing a path.

She saw Roan halt, his face rueful. Saw him look at her and shrug, his hands spread almost fatalistically, before he turned to face the newcomer.

A tall man was striding towards them, swarthily handsome, his powerful frame expensively clothed, his black hair grizzled with silver. Two other men followed, hurrying a little as if caught in his slipstream.

'Roan, *mou*. So you have won.' The man gestured round him. 'I salute your triumph, even if it has broken my heart. And I shall keep my word—and the terms of our wager. If painting is to be your life, I must accept that.'

Roan stayed where he was, smiling faintly, his head flung back. He said quietly, 'You are generous, Papa, but also mistaken. Our bet stated that I must arrange for an exhibition of my work to be staged within a year entirely by my own efforts. But that is not the case.

'Tonight's success was gained for me only with the help of Harriet, my wife. I could not have done it without her, so I lose our bet. Accordingly, I shall be returning with you to Greece to take up my position within the corporation as your heir.'

He walked across to Harriet, took her hand, and led her forward. 'Harriet this is my father, Constantine Zandros.'

He added into a silence suddenly as ominous as the lull before a thunderstorm, 'Papa, please greet your daughter, and give our marriage your blessing.'

CHAPTER TEN

'So, MY son too has taken an English bride.' Constantine Zandros spoke slowly, but his smile did not reach his eyes as he studied Harriet. 'Forgive me if I seem surprised.'

Surprised, thought Harriet, did not begin to describe her own sensations. She felt dazed, her mind reeling, as if she'd been sandbagged. Trapped in a nightmare which would not be forgotten in the morning.

And thankful, too, that she was sitting down, otherwise she'd probably have collapsed on the floor by now.

Outside in the gallery, the clearing up process was well under way, after the triumphs and sensations of the evening. Now she was here, in Desmond Slevin's office, away from any remaining prying eyes and ears eager for further revelations.

Roan stood beside her, his hand resting on her shoulder, and Gregory Flint was occupying another chair close to the door.

While Constantine Zandros sat behind the desk, like a judge presiding over a tribunal.

He went on, 'Why was I not informed of this marriage until now?'

Roan said evenly, 'The terms of the bet also stipulated no contact between us until it had been won or lost.'

'But the wedding of the Zandros heir should be a great occasion—a major celebration. Not a thing of haste and secrecy. Unless,' his father added slowly, 'it became necessary because you had allowed your ardour to outweigh your judgement and honour.' He paused. 'Is that how it was, my son? Are you and your English girl making me a grandfather? Is that why you felt obliged to marry her?'

Harriet was aware of her grandfather stiffening, his brows drawing together, and moved restively. Roan's hand tightened warningly on her shoulder.

He said softly, 'Papa, I saw her and wanted her. There was no more to it than that. And, naturally, I wished to claim her as my bride—mine and mine alone, before you think of asking,' he added with a significance that brought sudden colour into Harriet's white face. 'And just as soon as it could be arranged.'

His tone took on a note of challenge. 'You, of all people, must remember how that is.'

'Yes,' his father said shortly. 'Also how it can end.' He sighed angrily. 'I had my own plans for your future—a good Greek wedding to a suitable Greek wife. Someone to manage your home, behave with discretion, and give you strong children.' He gave Harriet's slender body a disparaging look. 'Can she even cook the food you like, this bride of yours?'

'No,' Roan said calmly. 'But as I have a chef, the need will not arise, so stop trying to frighten her. She is already struggling to accept that I am not the penniless artist she believed.'

'You tell me she never suspected that you were wealthy?' The older man snorted. 'Impossible.'

'On the contrary, she offered me financial support,' Roan retorted. 'I found it a refreshing change.'

'But you, *kyrie*, you must have known.' Constantine Zandros turned his frowning gaze on Gregory Flint.

'I knew Roan was not what he seemed,' Mr Flint agreed quietly.

'Yet you still encouraged this match?'

'I neither encouraged nor discouraged. They are grown-up people able to decide their own fates.'

There was a heavy silence, then Constantine Zandros sighed. 'Well, what is done cannot be undone without trouble and expense. Therefore I too must—accept.'

'Thank you.' Harriet spoke for the first time, her voice shaking. 'And now if you've all finished—dissecting me, I'd like to go home, please.'

'Yes, of course.' Her father-in-law inclined his head. 'Roan, take

your wife to the hotel, if you please, then send the car back for me.
I think Kyrios Flint and I should talk a little.'

'Hotel?' Harriet repeated blankly. 'What hotel? You don't
understand—I want to go back to my flat.' Her voice rose a little.
'My own place.' And felt once again Roan's hand tightening on
her shoulder.

There was a pause, then her grandfather spoke, his voice chilly
with disapproval. 'My dear Harriet, what is this nonsense? You seem
to have forgotten that your place is with your husband. Quite naturally, he and his father will have things they wish to discuss later,
so the hotel is the obvious choice. Now, away with you, and no more
arguments,' he added briskly. 'And I'll see you tomorrow.'

She got to her feet. She said desperately, grabbing at any excuse,
'But I can't stay at a hotel—not like this.' She gestured helplessly
at the ivory dress. 'Not without a change of clothes for the morning,
or a toothbrush. And my pyjamas.'

A reluctant smile touched the corners of Constantine's mouth.
'Your wife seems unduly modest, my dear Roan.' He looked at
Harriet. 'But the Titan Palace should be able to supply most of your
requirements, my child, or I shall wish to know why. And your
husband can deal with—' he waved a hand '—the other details.'

The Titan Palace. She said hoarsely, 'My God, it belongs to you,
doesn't it? The whole Titan Group.' She turned on Roan. 'And that's
why they were falling over themselves to serve us that afternoon.
Because someone recognised you.'

'You have visited my hotel?' Constantine asked, brows raised.

'By coincidence, some of our courtship took place there,' Roan said
silkily. 'But only in the lounge. Harriet has yet to see the bedrooms.'

His father gave a boom of laughter, and slapped him on the
shoulder. 'Then show them to her, my son, without delay. I will allow
you sufficient time for the pair of you to make a prolonged discov-
ery of their comforts.'

She walked beside Roan out of the office, and out of the gallery,
her head high, but her face scarlet with anger and embarrassment.

A car, large, dark and luxurious, was waiting at the kerb for
them, with a uniformed driver holding open the rear passenger door.

Harriet took her seat in icy silence, and sat rigidly waiting for Roan to join her.

As the car moved off, she said hoarsely, 'You stood there, and you let this happen. Without a bloody word. How could you? My God, are you that afraid of your father?'

'My father?' he bit back. 'How does this concern him? Tonight, I thought, was about your grandfather, and this on-going deception that you so cleverly devised. You asked me to help—to continue to play a part that already wearies me—and I did so.

'But what do I hear from you? "My flat—my pyjamas".' His mimicry was scornful. 'Your performance, Harriet *mou*, would not fool a small child. Both he and Papa must already be wondering what kind of marriage this really is.'

He shook his head. 'My father, of course, will not care. I tell you now he is simply waiting for it to end in divorce. No doubt he already has a suitable heiress in prospect for me.'

He paused for a moment, then continued grimly, 'But your grandfather's case is different. So, for the time being, just remember that becoming my wife was your own idea, and grit your teeth for the remainder of our time together.

'Unless this house of yours is no longer important to you,' he added. 'If so, confess the entire scheme to your grandfather, and end this farce now.'

She found herself wanting to shrink back into her corner of the car. To cover her ears against the relentless barrage of words, and the force behind them of anger, coldly controlled.

'No,' she said in a stifled voice. 'Gracemead still means—everything.'

He shrugged. 'Then we will go on with our pretence. Here—and in Greece.'

He heard her sharp, indrawn breath, and nodded. 'Yes, you are coming with me. What other choice do you have? Or are you crazy enough to think that your grandfather would accept a marriage conducted in different countries? Because I know he would not.'

'But I can't leave England.' She was trembling all over, her voice husky, pleading. 'I have a career—a life.'

He said softly, 'I thought you were prepared to sacrifice anything for that—heap of stone in the countryside.'

She didn't look at him. 'And I thought I'd already done so.'

'Well, you will not be called on to pay that particular price a second time.' There was a note in his voice she did not recognise. 'You have at last managed to convince me, *matia mou*, that I can expect nothing from you as my wife, and I shall not ask again.'

She bit her lip. 'What about my job?'

'You leave. I am sure your grandfather will clear the way for you.'

'Yes,' she agreed bitterly. 'Almost certainly. And my—the flat?'

'I imagine a tenant can be found until your return. I regret that we must share a house while you remain in Greece,' he added, after a pause. 'But it contains enough rooms to ensure your privacy. And when the time comes for us to divorce, I will supply all the necessary evidence, so that no blame can be attached to you.'

'Thank you,' she said. 'I believed until this evening that you were already doing so.'

He shrugged. 'You were so ready to think the worst of me that I decided to indulge you.'

'At your cousin's expense?' she queried tautly.

'You underestimate Lucy's sense of humour,' Roan retorted.

'And you overestimate mine,' Harriet said harshly. 'I can't believe that sane people would do this. My life turned upside down—wrecked—and all for a bloody bet. Show me the fun side of that.'

'You have your own agenda, Harriet *mou*, which I too find less than amusing. Besides, this thing with my father was more than just a bet.' His voice was weary. 'It was the resolution of a series of disagreements, which had become steadily more serious. I needed to establish my independence. Prove that I was my mother's son as well. That I loved and valued her memory, and her heritage, and would not allow it to be—airbrushed out of existence.'

'And what happens to that heritage now?' she demanded hotly. 'I—I thought you were a painter. You made me believe in you—Desmond Slevin too. He backed you, and you're leaving him in the lurch.'

'No,' he said. 'He has done well tonight, and that will not be the end of it. I made it clear to him at the beginning that painting could not be my full-time career. I am too much a Zandros for that. I want to run the corporation when my father decides to stand down. There are people all over the world who will be relying on me to make sure that we prosper, and that they continue to have work. I wish to take on those responsibilities, even—to make a difference. Believe that it is no way a hardship for me.' For a moment, his voice deepened passionately.

There was a pause, then he went on, more slowly, 'But I shall continue to paint in whatever leisure I have, and show my work through the Parsifal. Kyrios Slevin accepts that. And so must you, while you remain my wife.'

She said stonily, 'Which hopefully will not be for very long.'

'Amen to that,' he threw back harshly, and they sat in silence, side by side but miles apart, until they reached the Titan Palace.

Where the reality of being Roan Zandros' wife was brought home to Harriet with telling emphasis, by the awed greeting from the manager, the reverence with which he bowed over Harriet's startled hand, and how he himself ushered them into a high-speed lift to be whisked upwards.

'My father and his staff have commandeered the penthouse,' Roan told her, his face and tone expressionless. 'So we have been assigned the bridal suite. I hope that pleases you, my darling.'

Harriet made a sound that might have been interpreted as a gasp of approval, or even someone choking on her own fury.

They were shown into a luxurious sitting room, ablaze with flowers, its lights discreetly lowered. A side table held a basket of fruit, and an ice bucket, containing a bottle of champagne.

As Harriet gazed round her, there was a knock at the door, and the manager darted over to admit a waiter with a trolley, bearing pots of tea, coffee and hot chocolate, plus, under a domed glass cover, an array of the delicious sandwiches she remembered from her previous visit.

'My God,' she said when the manager eventually bowed himself out. 'They don't leave much to chance.'

'Perhaps they feel that honeymoon couples need to keep up their strength,' Roan returned, helping himself to smoked salmon sprinkled with caviare. 'May I get you something?'

'No,' she said. 'Thank you.'

'You express your gratitude in a manner all your own, Harriet *mou*.' He poured a cup of coffee. 'As if you were consigning me to be burned in hell.'

'If you want me to be grateful,' she said stormily, 'find us some way out of this appalling mess.'

'The situation is entirely of your own making.' He sounded bored. 'You seem to forget that. But it is not permanent. Be content with that.'

'You should have warned me,' she said. 'Told me that your father was coming.'

'I did not know it myself until this afternoon.' Roan grimaced. 'He was sent an invitation, but I never thought he would accept. I should have remembered that Papa enjoys the unexpected,' he added dryly.

'Not always.' She swallowed. 'Judging by his reaction to me.'

He put down his cup, and walked across to her, his fingers tipping up her chin so that he could look into her face. 'That hurt you?'

For a moment, the breath caught in her throat. 'No, why should it?'

'I cannot think of a single reason.' He let his hand drop, and turned away. 'And now I must go and meet with him. Try to convince him, among other things, that you and I adore each other. It will be an uphill struggle.' He pointed at a door on the other side of the room. 'The bedroom is there. I hope you find everything you need—apart, I fear, from pyjamas. The hotel's boutique does not stock them, and all the stores are closed now.'

She stared at him. '*The* bedroom? You mean there's just one?'

'With one bed.' He shrugged. 'I told you, *agapi mou*. It's the bridal suite, so we must make the best of it.' His brief smile held no humour. 'Comfort yourself that we are no longer bride and groom,' he added, and left.

One bed, Harriet thought, surveying it a few minutes later. But quite the largest she'd ever seen—and probably double the size of her own at the flat. And, quite simply, a wide, yielding, sexy playground. Or, perhaps, a space to be lost in and never found. Although she didn't derive much comfort from either notion.

However, in the beautifully fitted bathroom she found identical robes made of thick towelling, hanging behind the door. She showered quickly, uneasily aware that Roan might return at any moment, then wrapped herself securely in one of them, knotting the sash round her waist.

There were no books to be seen, she thought, as she got into bed. Presumably the suite's usual occupants were expected to have better things to do than read.

She moved her pillows as near to the edge of the bed as they would go without falling off, and pulled the covers discreetly up to her chin.

And the wisest policy now was to go to sleep, she thought, closing her eyes determinedly. But how could she relax when the truth was that she was waiting on tenterhooks for Roan's return?

Eventually, a long time later, she heard the door of the suite open and close, and then the sound of him quietly entering the bedroom. Walking over, she knew, to the bed, and looking down at her.

Keeping her eyes tightly closed, she attempted to breathe slowly and evenly.

'You are no actress, Harriet *mou*,' he commented mockingly. He took the edge of the sheet, and pulled it down a little, then gasped. 'You intend to wear that tonight?' His voice was incredulous. 'You will suffocate.'

She grabbed back the sheet, glaring at him. 'Even so, it's marginally better than the alternative.'

His mouth twisted. 'I hope you do not expect me to follow your example.' He walked towards the bathroom, pulling off his clothes as he went, and dropping them on the floor behind him.

Harriet turned hurriedly on to her stomach, and buried her face in the pillow, ashamed of the swift nervous surge the sight of him had engendered, bordering, she recognised, on—excitement.

He said he wouldn't ask again, she remembered, swallowing. But how much trust could she place in his assurances after that—that other time?

That first time…

Suddenly memories were stirring, unbidden and full force, and in their wake, at their prompting, came something more potent, and infinitely more dangerous.

Because her skin was tingling as if responding to the stroke of his hands, her lips softening and parting. Against the restriction of the towelling, her nipples were awakening to aching life.

She seemed to feel again the graze of his mouth touching every part of her body in sensual exploration. To know the sweet, searing flame of his tongue between her slackened thighs lifting her powerfully, irresistibly once more to the agonised tumult of climax.

She gasped convulsively, pressing her fist against her teeth, as she fought for control.

I don't want to feel like this, she told herself feverishly. *I dare not.*

And yet I want him so much I could die, and I can't go on fighting it, not while there's even a chance…

She sat up, wriggling out of the bathrobe, and tossing it away from her, so that it landed, quite deliberately, in the middle of the floor where he'd be bound to see it. Then she slid back under the sheet, turning on her side and adjusting her pillows to a more inviting distance.

He might not want to ask, she thought, but maybe—just maybe— he could be tempted…

It seemed for ever before she heard him emerge from the bathroom. Became aware that he was pausing briefly, then moving again, crossing towards the bed. Halting to switch off the lights, so that the room was plunged into semi-darkness, illumined only by the lights of the city penetrating the window drapes.

She felt the bed dip under his weight, and, hardly breathing, waited for him to reach for her. And waited…

When at long last she risked a fleeting glance over her shoulder, she could see him quite clearly, lying quietly, his hair black against the pillow, and the long, naked line of his back turned indifferently towards her.

In a silent rejection that brooked no appeal.

Making her realise she should have stayed, alone and lonely, in her self-imposed exile at the edge of the mattress. Forcing her to discover the hard way how difficult it was to cry, to feel the tears burning your face without moving, or making a sound, because the man you wanted was lying just an arm's length away, and might hear you.

Knowing that, if he did, you would never recover from the shame of it.

And wondering how you would ever be able to bear all the nights that were to come, until this mockery of marriage ended?

CHAPTER ELEVEN

THE light, Harriet thought, was amazing, with a clarity and intensity she'd never experienced before. But then, she reminded herself ironically, she'd never been to Greece before. Never even contemplated a holiday there, because all her vacation time was spent at Gracemead.

And certainly never imagined she'd be arriving anywhere by executive jet.

Leaving the airport for the chauffeur-driven car which was to take them down to the Militos peninsula, she felt as if she'd walked headlong into a wall of heat, and was thankful that the waiting vehicle had air-conditioning.

Roan, she'd gathered, usually made the transfer by helicopter, but this time he'd decided that Harriet should enjoy a more leisurely approach to her new home. If 'enjoy' was really the word, she thought, biting her lip.

She knew a little of what to expect. Two headlands jutting into the Aegean, Roan had told her, like long arms enclosing a small but beautiful bay. And on each arm—a house, facing each other, but separate.

'Rather like ourselves, *matia mou*,' he'd added, his tone faintly jeering.

And the bay, she thought. Does it have a flat rock with a table and chairs where people sit, drinking wine before they part in anger? And do you have other more pleasurable memories of it?

And did not ask.

But it was a relief to know she wouldn't be sharing a roof with Constantine Zandros. His stay in London had only been brief, but she'd still found his narrow-eyed scrutiny, and habit of firing questions at her, distinctly unnerving.

On his father's departure, Roan had arranged for them to move out of the bridal suite, where she'd had to spend two more supremely awkward nights, lying, with her back turned to him, on the furthest edge of that huge bed, and into the penthouse where at least she'd had a room to herself.

'But why can't I go back to my flat?' she'd queried rebelliously.

'Because the newspapers are still interested in our story,' Roan told her curtly. 'Do you want them camped on your doorstep day and night, or would you prefer the hotel press office to deal with them while you stay here, shielded by our security?'

She bit her lip. 'I'll stay here.'

Not that there'd been much time to worry about lurking cameramen. She'd spent those final days in England feeling as if she was caught up in a tidal race—swept ruthlessly along against her will, as her life was swiftly and efficiently dismantled.

She had never gone back to Flint Audley. Instead, her desk had been cleared, and its contents delivered to the hotel, while a different company was handling the letting of her flat.

Sometimes she'd managed to make a stand, insisting on buying her own clothes in department stores rather than the salons of major designers, choosing classic styles and fabric in cool, light colours. Keeping it all simple—things she could still use as soon as all this was behind her.

After all, she could well afford to do so, she thought. The cheque she'd paid Roan on their wedding day had been returned to her without comment. Just another business transaction.

And she'd also adamantly refused all Roan's attempts to buy jewellery for her.

'I'm not a child,' she'd told him defiantly, 'to be placated with meaningless glitter. Indulge your next wife instead. She'll need something to compensate for being the resident breeding machine.'

For a moment, his mouth had tightened dangerously, but all he'd said was, 'An unattractive thought, Harriet *mou*, unattractively expressed,' before turning away without another word.

Leaving her with the knowledge that she was in the wrong. She wasn't even sure why she'd succumbed to such childish rudeness, especially when Roan was clearly doing his best to be considerate. Except—it would be so easy to respond to his kindness and generosity, she realised wistfully. To let herself warm to his charm, yield to the sensuous pull of his attraction, and ignore its dangers. And to forget, perhaps fatally, the only reason this marriage had ever come about.

Gracemead...

The reason they'd married. And the sole reason they were still together.

She'd gone down to the house alone to say goodbye to her grandfather, expecting an emotional encounter, but instead she'd found Gregory Flint in robust mood, far readier to talk about the garden than her imminent departure.

'Aren't you going to miss me even a little?' she'd asked eventually, trying to smile.

'I imagine, my dear, that we shall miss each other.' He'd patted her shoulder. 'But you belong now with the man you've chosen, and I cannot be selfish. Besides,' he'd added, 'you're hardly moving to the dark side of the moon. And your father-in-law has kindly invited me to stay with him in Greece whenever I wish.'

He chuckled. 'Your husband has also reminded me that we still have a chess issue to resolve.'

'But I'll be coming back here too—for visits. Won't I?' There was a note of pleading in her voice.

And not just to visit, but to claim my inheritance. Because I did what you wanted, Grandfather. I—I married, and within the deadline you set, so when do I get my promised reward? When are you going to tell me that Gracemead is mine?

'I'm sure you will.' Gregory Flint gave her a brisk smile. 'But first you must give yourself time to adapt to your new life—your new environment. After all, your priority now, my dear, must be making a home for your husband.'

'I think he has servants to do that.' His evasion of the issue made her respond waspishly, and she saw him frown.

He said repressively, 'We are hardly speaking of the same thing,

Harriet.' He paused. 'Rust has been such a problem with the roses this year. I'm not sure the new sprays are as effective as the old ones were.'

And that, Harriet thought wearily, had been the end of that discussion, with no guarantees to comfort her, or even a hint of his intentions.

It had been Roan who'd organised a farewell dinner with Tessa and Bill, skilfully soothing their hurt feelings over the secret wedding by citing mysterious family reasons, then winning them over completely with an invitation to visit Militos before the summer was over.

'Is a stream of visitors really such a good idea?' she'd queried as they'd driven back to the hotel. 'Couldn't it be—awkward?'

'Why, *matia mou*,' he'd drawled, 'are you saying you'd prefer to be alone with me?'

Which had silenced her.

There'd been an even trickier meeting with Jack and Lucy. The other girl had been polite but chilly, so perhaps she hadn't thought the supposed affair funny after all. But when they'd briefly been alone, and Harriet had attempted a stumbling apology, Lucy had brusquely cut across her.

'Do you think I care about that nonsense? The truth is I can't bear to think of Roan, the guy I love best in the world after Jack and my father, throwing himself away on someone who doesn't give a damn about him.' She'd shaken her head. 'What a waste. What a bloody waste.'

But you don't understand, Harriet had wanted to scream at her. I saw you that day because I was desperate for him—because I couldn't bear to stay away any longer. Hearing about Tessa's baby had started me thinking in ways I'd never known—about things I couldn't afford to want. Stupid, unrealistic dreams that are not—*not*—part of my plan, and can never be, because they'll ruin everything.

Aloud, she'd said quietly, 'It won't last long, and then he'll have his life back. We both will.' And walked away.

Remembering, Harriet suppressed a sigh. Today should have been wonderful, she thought, staring out of the window at the rich earth colours of the parched summer landscape, the greys and violets of distant hills, and the silvery masses of the olive groves that lined the road. A fairy tale—Cinderella travelling to her palace, her prince at her side—instead of a situation rife with potential for disaster. If she wasn't careful.

Because she didn't belong here, and she must never forget that for a moment. Not that her father-in-law would permit her to, she reminded herself wryly.

She turned to Roan to make some bright, innocuous comment about the landscape, only to find his attention obviously riveted elsewhere. And, following the direction of his gaze, Harriet saw with vexation that the brief skirt of her pale yellow dress had ridden up, exposing a length of slender thigh.

She made a hasty adjustment, tugging her skirt down to her knees, and saw his mouth curl in swift derision.

'Harriet, I have seen every inch of you naked, so spare us both the token gesture.' He spoke with cool emphasis. 'And if I wish to look at your charming legs, I shall do so, because I am reminded there was once a time when they were wrapped round my waist—to our mutual enjoyment.'

Her face burned, and she said imploringly, 'Roan—please. The driver will hear…'

'Yanni does not speak English,' he retorted. He pushed her skirt almost casually back to its previous level, letting his hand rest lightly just above her knee. 'And don't flinch, *agapi mou*,' he added mockingly. 'As my wife, you should be accustomed to my touch by now. Should even welcome it.'

She sat rigidly, not looking at him, staring at the passing scenery with eyes that saw nothing. Roan might choose to play games, but she would not—could not—let them get to her.

'We shall be reaching the village quite soon,' he said, after a pause. 'And we are expected, so try to smile, *pedhi mou*. Be the happy bride they want to see.'

'In that case, perhaps you'd remove your hand.'

His mouth tightened, but he did as she asked, as the car began its descent into the village.

Harriet thought he'd exaggerated, yet it seemed as if the entire population had turned out to mark their progress through the narrow streets, beaming with delight and waving, forcing a shy response from her in turn.

Yanni turned with a flash of white teeth, calling something, and Roan shrugged, spreading his hands and laughing back at him.

'What did he say?' Harriet asked.

'You really wish to know?' His glance was sardonic. 'He was suggesting that as we robbed them of a wedding, we should not keep them waiting to celebrate the christening.'

Which serves me right for asking, Harriet thought, subsiding into fresh embarrassment.

Then the car turned a corner, and suddenly the sea was in front of them, a sheet of exquisite blue glass in the windless afternoon, blending seamlessly with the sky in a distant shimmering haze of heat.

She said on a sigh, all other considerations momentarily forgotten, 'Oh, God, that's so—incredibly beautiful.'

'Yes,' Roan said quietly. 'And each time I see it is like the first.'

'But you must surely be used to it.'

'As I told you, I spent most of my childhood in England with my mother. Until I returned, I had almost forgotten what it meant to me—that it was in my blood and always would be.'

She forced a smile. 'I—I know the feeling.' And was aware of his dry glance.

They traversed the small harbour, with its bobbing *caiques*, then turned inland again, the road climbing. In the distance, Harriet could see a sprawl of white walls topped in terracotta.

'The Villa Dionysius,' Roan said. 'Where my father lives. You will find that I have built on a smaller scale—but with room for expansion.'

'When you become domesticated? The settled family man?' She made her voice light and cool, even faintly scathing, to cover the pain that had come from nowhere to twist inside her at the thought of Roan with his firstborn in his arms. *A baby that she had not given him...*

No, she castigated herself. Stop right now. Because you cannot—must not go there. It—it's just not safe.

She managed a laugh. 'I find that hard to imagine.'

He said quietly, 'My friends who have children might not agree with you, Harriet *mou*,' and turned away from her.

She could see the other headland now, just as he'd described. Could observe that the house was single-storeyed, built on three sides, with a roof tiled in dark green.

'Welcome to your home, Harriet *mou*.' His voice was almost expressionless. 'And prepare yourself to be adored.'

For a moment his words startled her, then she saw the group of people waiting in high excitement to greet them at the main entrance, and understood.

She said, half to herself, 'I feel such a fraud. I don't think I can do this.'

'You wish to go back to England? Tell your grandfather the truth?'

'No—he'd be so disappointed in me. I can't do that to him.'

Roan said with sudden harshness, 'Then please do not distress my people with your honesty either.'

As the car came to a halt, he leaned forward. 'The man in the grey linen jacket is Panayotis. He manages the house for me, does the hiring, orders the supplies—everything. He speaks good English, and you may rely on him completely.

'The woman next to him, almost dancing, is Toula, my house-keeper.' He paused. 'She was also my nurse when I was born, and because of this, like Yanni and the villagers, she may have certain—hopes of this marriage. Try to be patient with her.'

She said bitterly, 'How to feel guilty in one easy lesson. You should have left me in England.'

'Yes,' he said curtly. 'But perhaps I too wished to spare your grandfather's feelings. Shall we go?'

Harriet felt hideously self-conscious as the introductions were made. The smiles did not waver, but she could sense the surprise behind them, and knew she was not the glowing, beautiful bride they'd anticipated.

Takis, the portly chef, already seemed to be running a measuring glance over her slenderness, the light of battle in his bright eyes.

And she was briefly aware of one openly disparaging glance emanating from a ravishingly pretty girl, full-lipped and sloe-eyed, who was standing at the back of the group.

Perhaps she was hoping to catch the master's eye herself, Harriet thought dryly, and thinks I've spiked her guns.

Roan was talking to Panayotis. 'All the work I ordered has been completed, I hope?'

'*Ne, kyrie.*' Panayotis nodded vigorously in confirmation. 'The men finished two days ago, and the new furnishings came yesterday. Everything is ready for your bride.'

'Shall we take a look, *agapi mou*?' Roan's arm was round her waist, urging her forward, but at least he wasn't carrying her across the threshold.

'You've been having alterations done already?' It was infinitely cooler inside the villa, where massive fans hung from the ceilings, and the light was beguilingly dim, thanks to the shutters drawn across the windows, filtering out the immediate fierceness of the sunlight.

Looking round, Harriet approved of the immaculate walls washed in clear pastel colours, and the marble floors which emphasised the same sense of space and peace she'd aimed for in her London flat. However, here any starkness was relieved by the rich greens and ochres of the fabrics—by lamps and ceramics—by clusters of books and magazines, and masses of greenery. The organised clutter of everyday living.

She added with bewilderment, 'But the place looks brand-new.'

'I decided that the main bedroom needed some refurbishment.' Roan smiled at her. 'Now that I am no longer a bachelor. Shall we take a look?'

'If—if you want.' Her voice sounded hollow, matching the panicky sensation inside her, as Panayotis led the way, beaming, down a wide passageway to double doors at the end.

'You see, *kyrie*,' he announced proudly, flinging them wide.

The shutters were open, and the room was flooded with light. As she hesitated in the doorway, half dazzled, she received a confused impression of pale walls warmed with a hint of apricot—gauzy drapes framing the enormous window with its stunning view of the sea—and a vivid splash of blue silk, the same deep colour as the Aegean itself, lying across the foot of the big bed facing the door.

Yet it was the scent that Harriet really noticed—a heavy, cloying fragrance that seemed to fill the air, and make it difficult to breathe.

Somewhere near at hand, she heard someone gasp, and then as

she took a step further into the room, she saw for the first time what was also on the bed, propped up in the centre of the mountain of snowy pillows, and the remaining breath left her lungs completely.

It was the unframed portrait of a woman lying on her side, her head resting on her folded arms, and one leg slightly drawn up. A very beautiful woman with hair so fair it was almost silver, and cropped close to emphasise the elegant shape of her skull. A woman with slanting dark eyes in an olive-skinned face as pointed as a cat's, her curved crimson mouth smiling an invitation that was so smoulderingly, blatantly explicit that she did not actually need to be nude.

Yet she was naked, just the same, every line of her perfect body glowing from the canvas, provocative and unashamed.

And there was no possible doubt about the identity of the artist who'd brought her so sensually alive. One glance told her that, because Harriet now recognised his style as immediately as she knew the face she saw in the mirror each morning.

She was aware of a subdued shocked murmur from the servants crowding into the doorway behind her—of Panayotis moving forward, his face an image of disbelief—of Toula giving a little wail as she threw the skirt of her white apron over her head.

She turned slowly and looked at Roan. He was standing, hands on hips, head tilted almost critically, regarding the canvas as if he was considering what improvements he could make to the composition.

And as she stared at him, she saw his mouth curve faintly into amusement, as if he was also enjoying some agreeable memory. Recalling a time, no doubt, when the girl lying across his bed had been flesh and blood, and not merely an arrangement of tones.

Suddenly Harriet found herself remembering the sketch he'd done of her. A cross between a witch and a bat, she thought, faintly nauseated as another wave of that overwhelming perfume reached her. Could there be a greater contrast?

He wanted me for one night, she told herself, because I was his virgin bride, and therefore a novelty. But how often has he made love here in this room with his silver-haired beauty? The room where I'm supposed to sleep alone, and in that same bed…

With his—welcome home gift hanging on the wall for company.

Misery rose in her, in a great swamping, choking rush. Anger too, and humiliation as she thought of his smile, and knew she could never compete with that kind of memory.

She took a step forward. 'You find this amusing.' Her voice shook. 'Well, I don't.' She swung back her hand and slapped him hard across the face.

Then she turned and ran, the sea of stunned faces parting for her.

CHAPTER TWELVE

ROAN caught her easily—for one thing she had no idea where she was going—his hand descending like a clamp on her shoulder, as he pushed her into the nearest room. Swung her to face him in its shuttered dimness.

'How dare you?' His voice was molten. 'How dare you shame me like that in front of my household?'

'I think their sympathies might rest with me.' She tried for defiance, wrenching herself from his grasp. 'What was it, Roan—a belated wedding present? You might have warned me what to expect. And how to react.'

She adopted a brittle drawl. 'How fascinating, darling. From your early period, I suppose. Someone else whose every inch you once had cause to study. Forgive me if I find the overall effect rather too exotic—like her perfume.' She drew a harsh breath. 'Is that better?'

'Take care, Harriet *mou*,' he said harshly. 'Or you might begin to sound like a jealous woman.'

Her heart seemed to twist. 'Hardly,' she returned. 'I made it clear from the start that I wouldn't interfere in your private life. I just didn't bargain for finding it—in my face. I had hoped you'd be more discreet.'

She looked away. 'Maybe you should tell me her name, in case I suddenly encounter her leaving your bedroom one of these days, and need to say Good morning.'

'Her name is Ianthe Dimitriou,' he said. 'And you will not meet her in this house, or, I hope, anywhere else. She belongs in the past, and what has happened today means nothing.'

How can you say that, she asked silently, when I'm standing here—dying inside? I believed I'd suffered thinking of you with Lucy, but I knew nothing—*nothing*…

'But she was—your mistress?' Even asking these things was like stabbing herself repeatedly with a knife, she thought. A pain she must submit to. And at any moment the blood might flow.

'Of course.' He sounded impatient. 'Harriet, if I had wished to lead a celibate life, I would have entered a monastery. You knew there had been other women in my life before we met, so do not pretend.'

'Pretence seems to have become second nature to me.' She looked around her at the shadowy room, absorbing the details of a bed made up with a striped cover, a chest of drawers, a fitted closet, and a half-open door which clearly led into a bathroom. 'But I find I have my limits. So, I'll be sleeping in here tonight, and all the nights to come while I remain here.'

She lifted her chin. 'In one way, your Ianthe has done me an enormous favour. After her intervention, no one will question that we're—estranged. Problem solved.'

'You are wrong,' he said. 'At this moment, everyone in the house believes that we are on that bed together, enjoying a passionate re-conciliation. And that, after I have atoned for my past sins with a suitably expensive gift, the incident will be forgotten, and you will take your place as my dutiful and adoring wife.

'And that, *matia mou*,' he added softly, 'is exactly how it will be, at least in the eyes of our small world. Only you and I will know the truth.'

'You think I'm going back to that room—under any circumstances?' She drew a ragged breath. 'I won't do it.'

'I think you will,' Roan told her with faint grimness. 'Unless you want me to make this physical reunion of ours a reality. Perhaps that would solve even more problems.'

He paused. 'Well?'

Harriet stared at the floor. 'I'll—sleep in the other room.'

'How disappointing.' She could hear the smile in his voice. Then he moved away, and presently she heard the creak of a mattress. She looked up, startled, and saw that Roan, his shoes and socks discarded, was stretched out on top of the bed.

'What are you doing?'

'Allowing some time to pass,' he said. 'After all, we are supposed to be making love, taking each other to paradise. Something unlikely to be achieved in a few minutes.' Reflectively, he folded his arms behind his head. 'Almost certainly you are making me plead a little first,' he went on. His mouth twisted wryly. 'But not too much, I hope.'

He glanced across at her. 'There is a chair, if you wish to sit while you are waiting. Or you could join me here.'

'The chair will be fine.' She sat down primly, knees and feet together like a schoolgirl. Minutes ticked by. The silence began to grow oppressive, or she found it so at least. Roan, on the other hand, seemed perfectly relaxed, almost as if he was on the brink of falling asleep.

She said, 'May I ask you something?'

'Anything.'

'Ianthe—how did you meet her?'

'She was staying further along the coast at the villa a friend of hers had rented for the summer. A woman called Maria Chrysidas. There was a party, and I was invited. Ianthe had learned somehow that I had ambitions to be a painter, and talked to me about art—asked if she could see my work.

'Accordingly, she came to my studio in the village the following day. She expressed her admiration for what I was trying to do, and suggested I should paint her. I had to explain I had little experience in portraiture.'

He paused. 'While I was explaining, she took off her clothes, and it seemed pointless to argue further.'

She took a breath. 'Were you in love with her?'

He said quite gently. 'You have seen her, Harriet *mou*. Let us say only that, at the time, she—suited my needs.'

'She's—incredibly beautiful.' She was proud of the steadiness in her voice. 'Had she done modelling before?'

'Probably. She was not shy about revealing herself,' he added dryly. 'But her real ambition, she told me, was to act. And, although she did not say so at first, to persuade me to use some of my money to finance her career.'

'And did you?'

'I might have done, but she made the mistake of letting me see her play a small role in a private production.' He sighed. 'She was— truly dreadful.'

He grinned suddenly. 'When I saw the bedroom today, it occurred to me that she might have been more successful off-stage as a set designer. But only with a suitable assistant to do the real work,' he added thoughtfully. 'Which makes me wonder which of the servants helped her.'

'Yet they all seemed so surprised,' Harriet pointed out. 'Perhaps she—slipped in while no one was looking.'

His mouth twisted. 'Carrying a large and awkward parcel to an unfamiliar house, and needing to find one specific room? I don't think so. She is spiteful, but not particularly ingenious. No, I believe she issued her instructions, leaving someone else to place her portrait in that particular way, and pour a bottle of her favourite scent all over the bed. Our bed, as she thought.'

He paused. 'I told Panayotis to burn all the bedding as well as the canvas.'

She said slowly, 'You're saying you never brought her here? How can that be when you were—involved?' She swallowed. 'Lovers.'

'We met elsewhere—at the studio—Maria's villa—my apartment in Athens. Also, I was travelling a good deal, and she went with me. But not here. I decided a long time ago, *pedhi mou*, that the only woman I would ever bring to my home would be my wife.'

She took a breath. 'But you used to be together down in the bay, surely? That was her shoe?'

'Yes. She lost it while flouncing off in temper.' He turned his head slowly and looked at her. 'Do you want to know why we quarrelled?'

'It's hardly my business…'

'You have made it so. And I have told you everything else, therefore if you mean yes, then say it.'

She bit her lip. 'All right, then. Yes.'

'I told her I was going to London to paint. I'd assumed she would wish to go with me. But when she found out there would be no first

class travel or five-star accommodation, and I would be living on what
I could earn, her passion for me waned with embarrassing speed.

'She still wanted my lifestyle, but not, it seemed, my life. I was
being selfish and a fool, she told me. If I wanted to indulge my little
hobby, why not California? As a celebrity painter, I could make
another fortune, and she could further her career at the same time.
She even hinted that we might get married.

'And why, she demanded, should I risk upsetting my father, who
had only just regained me as his son, when I might lose out on my
inheritance?

'Clearly she had her future all mapped out, and she was furious
with me for spoiling her plans. So, eventually I got angry too, for
thinking even for a second that she might want me more than my
bank balance.

'As we parted, she screamed I was a callous, unfeeling bastard,
and she would make me sorry one day.' He added wryly, 'Presumably,
this is the day she chose.' He felt the cheek Harriet had slapped with
his fingertips. 'I should hate to think there might be another.'

She said stiffly, 'I—I apologise for hitting you. I didn't understand.'

'*Endaxi.*' He sent her a brief smile. 'I too am sorry—that she will
have the satisfaction of knowing your reaction to her malice.'

There was a silence, then he said, 'Now will you tell me something?'

She was instantly on guard. 'Maybe. It depends.'

He said, 'Why do you never speak of your mother?'

Harriet bit her lip. 'I suppose my grandfather must have mentioned her—told you what happened.'

'He said she had left you in his care when you were a small child,
and that over the last few years all contact with her had been lost.'

Harriet nodded, not looking at him. 'The last address was somewhere in Argentina, but she replied to none of the letters that I—
that we sent. Of course, she might just have met someone
else—another man—and moved on. She tended to do that. There
were—always other men.'

'Is that why—for you—there were no men at all?'

He was too perceptive, she thought painfully. She lifted her chin.
'If that was true, I wouldn't be here.'

'Ah,' Roan said softly. 'But you are not really here. Not yet.' He paused. 'It might be possible to trace her.'

She gave a careful smile. 'A needle in a haystack, I'm afraid. Besides, if she ever wants to make contact, she knows where I'll be.'

He said gently, 'Is that why Gracemead is so important to you? Because it is the place where your mother left you, and where she might find you again—if she came back?'

'No,' she said. 'It's my home, just as this is yours. Nothing more. So forget any deep psychological reasoning.'

'As you wish.' With a slight shrug, Roan sat up. 'And now I think I have allowed sufficient time for us to have—renewed our marriage vows.' His tone was sardonic as he glanced at his watch. 'I shall tell Toula you are sleeping, and ask her to wake you in an hour with some coffee. So, when I go, take off your clothes and get into bed.'

'What for?'

His sigh was brief and impatient, as he reached for his shoes. 'Because I would hardly have made love to you with your clothes on.'

'Oh, I see,' she marvelled. 'It's to bolster your image as the great lover. Now, why should I wish to do that?'

'Because I have asked you to.' He swung himself off the bed, and walked towards her. He halted, his dark eyes scanning her face and travelling over her body, then suddenly pulled her towards him, his hands seeking the zip at the back of her dress, and tugging it downward.

He said silkily, 'But perhaps I should overcome your reluctance by reminding you, *agapi mou*, exactly how I can make you feel— if I wish.'

'No—please.' She clutched at the slipping dress in panic, as her whole body seemed to lurch in desire. 'I'll do what you say—when you've gone.'

'Another disappointment.' Roan's hand cupped the nape of her neck, his thumb slowly and deliberately caressing the side of her throat. He said softly, 'Have you never wondered, Harriet, if we might somehow rediscover what we shared on that magical night in London?'

Her heart missed a beat. 'Magical?' She managed scorn. 'Your description—not mine.' *And afterwards you—walked away...*

'Because I found it so,' he said. 'I even allowed myself to

dream—to hope that perhaps the joy we had known might change things between us. That you might find that you—wanted me. And that, if I was patient, you would come to me.'

His voice deepened. 'Do you know how many days and nights I waited, *matia mou*, before I gave up hoping?'

And I waited just forty-eight hours, she thought, only to find you with Lucy, and be saved from myself. I wish I could feel more grateful.

She said, 'Our marriage was a business arrangement. For me, that still applies.'

Roan released her abruptly. 'Then, as a matter of business, let us discuss how I can make amends for this traumatic homecoming— what form my penance should take.' His tone was silky. 'You don't want rubies or sapphires, so is there anything else you can suggest?'

'There's only one thing in the world I want,' she said coldly and clearly. 'And that, unfortunately, is not in your gift, or I would not have to be here.'

She added, 'And my real homecoming—to Gracemead—will be very different. I promise you that.'

He nodded, turning away. 'Then there is no more to be said,' he told her curtly over his shoulder, and went, leaving Harriet, standing alone in the shadows of the room, trembling suddenly, and close to tears.

'It's a question of survival,' she whispered into the silence. 'And I'll get through this—somehow, whatever it takes. And this will be my penance.'

Harriet replaced the cap on the sunblock, and lay back on her lounger with a sigh, listening to the soft whisper of the sea only yards away from her. It was just over half an hour from noon, and the heat was building in intensity.

'Don't be tempted to stay out in the middle of the day,' Roan had warned her. 'Protect your skin at all times, especially in the sea, and drink water constantly.'

She'd followed his advice, and so far remained unscathed. Or on the surface at least.

In spite of its past associations, she'd come to love this little beach, much preferring it to the hothouse atmosphere that often prevailed in the villa, she thought wryly. Since that first day, the staff had tended to tiptoe around her as if she was made of crystal.

She'd returned to the master bedroom, embarrassed to her soul to know what they must all be thinking, and found a transformation had been effected.

A thorough cleaning had taken place, and the glass doors on to the terrace had been flung wide to admit the sunlit air. In addition all the furniture had been moved around, so that the freshly made-up bed no longer faced the door. Leaving, she realised, not a trace of the scene—or the scent—that had greeted her on arrival.

And she'd discovered that the pretty, sullen-looking maid she'd noticed earlier had been summarily dismissed, after she'd tearfully confessed to Panayotis that she had smuggled in the portrait, and emptied that entire bottle of Summer Orchid over the *kyrie*'s bed, because the Kyria Dimitriou had promised to help her to a career as a model if she did so.

Poor kid, Harriet thought, with a sigh. And all to wreck a marriage that's on the rocks anyway.

She'd had to work hard to reassure Panayotis, who clearly blamed himself for his lack of vigilance.

'Never—never did I dream such a thing could happen,' he told her mournfully. 'Your own room, *kyria*, with everything that Kyrios Roan ordered to make it beautiful for you—the exquisite linen—that wonderful cover, handmade and embroidered in gold—all ruined. At least the new bed was spared.'

He threw his hands towards heaven. 'That creature—she should be taken out and whipped.'

'That's a bit harsh,' Harriet objected, startled. 'She's just young and silly.'

'No, *kyria*. Not Mitsa, who is indeed a fool. That other one.' He snorted contemptuously. 'Never would she accept that it was over— that her day was done. Always the letters—the telephone calls—even after Kyrios Roan had gone away. And when it was known he would return—daring to come here to his door—demanding to be admitted—to leave messages.'

He became belatedly aware that this might not be information his master's wife would welcome, and halted abruptly.

'And in the end, she succeeded,' Harriet said lightly. She forced a smile. 'And what a message. Not that it matters any more.'

Except that it did—*it did*…

Because it wasn't simply the bedroom that had changed. When she had next encountered Roan over dinner that night, it was to find he'd retreated behind an invisible wall of cool courtesy bordering on indifference.

The man who'd talked to her softly in the semi-darkness—who'd touched her with the hands of desire only an hour or so before—had somehow ceased to exist.

In his place was the polite stranger she was now learning to live with. Someone who spent as little time in her company as possible, refrained from any unnecessary physical contact, and carefully avoided all personal topics when they were obliged to talk to each other—usually over meals. At those times, he focussed on the political situation, regional agriculture, and the economics of tourism.

Sometimes, as she rose from the dining table, Harriet felt she could have answered a test paper on any of them.

She supposed she should have been reassured that he was no longer trying to persuade her to be his wife in any real sense. Instead, she found herself torn apart by the conflict in her emotions, bewildered—even scared—by the totally irrational joy that overwhelmed her when she saw him. Knowing it was only the fear of a rebuff that kept her from running to him, and throwing herself into his arms each time he returned home.

Aware that, on another level, she missed, inconsolably, the smile in his eyes, the warmth of his hand clasping hers, the softly spoken endearments that she knew meant nothing, yet somehow mattered so very much now that she no longer heard them.

Not that he was at home a great deal. She had soon learned that the Zandros Corporation was more than just a hotel chain, with far-reaching interests in shipping, industry and even farming. So, Roan's workload, since his return, had provided him with a perfect excuse to be elsewhere.

Not that she blamed him, Harriet thought, with another small sigh. In his place she would pick a hotel suite anywhere in the world over the narrow single bed in the adjoining dressing room where he spent his nights at the villa.

But when she'd suggested, stumbling a little, that he could not be comfortable, and there were surely—other rooms, knowing she was waiting with bated breath for his reply, he'd merely raised a cynical eyebrow.

'A small sacrifice in the cause of our supposed marital unity,' he'd drawled. 'And it will not be for ever.'

No, she'd thought, as she turned away. Nothing was. And that was her only comfort.

She picked up her watch from the table beside her lounger, and fastened it on her wrist, then collected the rest of her things together in her pretty raffia shoulder bag.

It was time she went indoors to get ready for the weekly ordeal of lunch with her father-in-law.

And what would be on today's menu? she wondered wryly, as she climbed the flight of shallow steps back to the garden. Her apparent inability to learn more than a few simple words in Greek was always a popular choice, as was her reluctance to mix with the other wives of wealthy men who lived around the peninsula. To join them for lunch, or coffee and sweet, sticky, pastries and admire their material possessions, and, where her own age group was concerned, their babies.

She bit her lip, knowing she was being unfair. That several of the younger women spoke good English, and that there were friendships to be made if she met them even halfway.

But shyness, and the constant awareness that her marriage existed on borrowed time, and she would soon be gone, held her back.

However, Constantine Zandros would probably opt for the latest bone of contention—the fact that she'd adamantly refused a party, complete with dancing, whole lambs roasted on spits, and guests invited from miles around, to celebrate her twenty-fifth birthday in a few days' time.

He had made his displeasure clear, and it had taken Roan's intervention, insisting coolly and firmly that his wife's wishes must be respected, for the matter to be closed.

If indeed it was. Constantine Zandros was not a man to readily accept defeat, she thought, biting her lip. And Roan was not around to defend her, having spent the past forty-eight hours in the Greek capital.

Showered and changed, she studied her reflection. Her dark green shift was modestly elegant, and complemented by her matching high-heeled sandals. Her lashes wore a coating of mascara, and her mouth was painted a soft coral, echoed in the polish on her toe and fingernails.

The image of a successful wife, she thought with irony, glancing across at the closed door which led to the dressing room, remembering how, for the first week, she'd lain awake at night, convinced that it would eventually open, and that Roan would come to her.

Do you know how many days and nights I waited, matia mou...?

His words haunted her, because now she'd experienced for herself the torment of waiting. Of feeling hope drift away.

Yet the increasing number of nights he spent away from home were even worse, because then she hardly slept at all, staring into the warm darkness, and weeping inside as she wondered if he was alone.

Wishing she'd had the courage back in London to tell him that she wanted him—that she needed him like the sun that warmed her and the breath that filled her lungs.

But she hadn't done so, she thought, picking up her broad-brimmed hat and her bag. Nor would she. Because their lives were set on completely different paths, and nothing could change that. Certainly nothing as ephemeral as physical desire, anyway.

Her car was waiting outside, the sleek, dark red, open-topped beauty that had suddenly appeared a couple of days after her arrival.

'My penance,' Roan had told her with a smile that did not reach his eyes. 'And your independence. Something that you will not refuse, I think.'

And had walked away while she'd tried to stammer her astonished gratitude, amazed that he'd known she even possessed a licence.

She'd been glad of it too, because it had enabled her to get away from the villa, and explore more of the peninsula. To visit churches, and wander round markets. To sit and drink coffee under faded awnings in small village squares, watching the local men playing endless games of backgammon, their fingers moving like lightning over the boards.

On a more practical level, the car spared her an otherwise lengthy walk to the Villa Dionysius, although she was sure a chauffeur-driven limousine would have been sent for her had she demurred even slightly.

My every wish granted, she thought with irony, except those that really matter.

Constantine Zandros was waiting for her on the broad terrace overlooking the sea, at a table set as usual in a vine-shaded pergola. His greeting was polite, but his gaze was critical as he handed her a glass of chilled wine.

'You have lost weight,' he commented. 'Do you not care for the food that your kitchen provides, or is it possible you are fretting over my son's constant absences?' he added with a cold smile.

Well, she hadn't seen that coming, Harriet thought, leaning back in her chair, her fingers tracing the stem of her glass.

'Roan takes his responsibilities very seriously,' she returned levelly. 'As you must be aware. I can hardly object to that. And Takis is a wonderful chef. Last night he served the most fabulous curry.'

He snorted. 'He should make you good Greek food—put flesh on your bones.'

He waited while two uniformed maids handed bread, then served the first course of peppers filled with a delicious mixture of minced, spiced meat and rice.

When they were alone, he went on, 'I had hoped that after his time in England I would now see more of my son, especially with a new wife to keep him at home. But I have been disappointed. As he is also, I think.' He paused. 'Perhaps if his bed was warmer, he would return more often,' he added significantly.

Harriet's fork clattered on to her plate. She met his impassive gaze, her face burning. 'What are you talking about? You know nothing…'

'But servants know everything,' he said. 'Also they gossip, and they say that you sleep alone. Is it true?'

She said chokingly, 'You have no right to ask such things…'

'No right to discuss the happiness of my only child?' he asked coldly. 'You are mistaken. Perhaps in your England it is not done to talk of such matters, but you are in my country now, and it is time that you recognised your duties as a wife. Time that you gave my son pleasure at night—and the promise of children. The things a man wants from his marriage.

'Because I tell you, girl, that if you continue to deny him, he will find consolation with someone else.'

He paused. 'So what is it with you? Are you still aggrieved over a foolish trick played by some slut from his past? Or do you not find him attractive?'

It wasn't easy to rally your defences when you were furiously angry, and blushing all over as well, but Harriet managed it.

She said curtly, 'Perhaps the boot's on the other foot, Kyrios Zandros. Maybe Roan no longer—wants me.'

'Then do something about it,' he said. 'After all, you are a woman, if thin. And a man has needs.' He gave her a cynical look. 'He does not have to be romantically in love in order to satisfy them. Or to satisfy the girl he takes.'

He uttered another snort. 'Pyjamas,' he added contemptuously.

Harriet pushed back her chair. She said tautly, 'I won't listen to any more of this.'

'Stay where you are. I have not much more to say.' He leaned forward, his gaze piercing her. 'I do not speak lightly, my girl. I too married an *anglithka* who did not want me, and she broke my heart. Do you imagine I wish to see my son suffer in the same way?' He banged his fist on the table. 'No and—no!' He took a deep breath, and drank some wine. 'Now, eat your food, and we will talk of other things. I heard today that your grandfather comes for your birthday.'

And that, Harriet thought almost faintly, is what they call a *volte face*. Making it impossible for her to tell him to go to hell and walk out. As he probably knew.

'That's wonderful news.' She forced herself to pick up her fork. Her voice sounded like broken glass. 'How did you persuade him to leave his beloved garden?'

'The garden?' The heavy brows rose. 'I thought it was the house—this Gracemead—that was so much to be desired.'

'Of course,' she said, wondering what Roan had been telling him. 'And the grounds—his flowers—are all part of that.'

'But they cannot mean more to him than you, the child of his blood. Therefore he will be here for your birthday. I have invited him to stay with me, and in the evening I shall give a dinner—ask our friends to meet him.' He paused. 'You cannot object to that, I hope?'

No, she thought, mentally gritting her teeth. I can't, you self-willed monster.

Aloud, she said expressionlessly, 'It will be delightful. Thank you.'

'You wish to show me gratitude, *pedhi mou*?' He smiled at her blandly. 'Then give me grandchildren.'

Always the last word, Harriet thought, seething, as she made herself resume eating. She picked at the lamb cutlets and green beans served as the next course, and chose a nectarine from the fresh fruit offered as dessert.

While they were drinking the thick, sweet Greek coffee which completed the meal, they heard the sound of an approaching helicopter and saw it swing in over the other headland, and descend.

'Ah, your husband returns,' Constantine Zandros commented with satisfaction. 'And you will be eager to welcome him home, I am sure, as a wife should. So do not let me detain you, daughter.'

Mute with rage, she left, swinging her car recklessly out of the gate. Fifty yards on, she braked, pulling over to the verge while she fought to regain her composure. Finding instead that she was going over the entire confrontation in her mind. Determining at the same time that it would be the first and last time he spoke to her in that way.

She resumed her short journey, driving with exaggerated care. She didn't want an accident before she'd given Roan a piece of her mind about his father's behaviour, and made it clear she wouldn't stand for it.

She left the car at the door, and marched in, heading for the master suite, but found only Toula there, unpacking his case in the dressing room.

'Oh.' Harriet checked. 'I—I was looking for Kyrios Roan.'

'He was here, *kyria*, but now he has gone out again.' Toula sounded reproachful. 'I think to the place where he paints.'

My studio in the village...

Harriet hesitated. 'Can you tell me how to find it, perhaps?'

'Of course, *kyria*.' Toula sounded surprised, as if she'd expected her young mistress to know already. 'It is near the harbour, on the upper floor of the house next to the Taverna Ariadne.' She hesitated. 'But he does not like to be disturbed there.'

An unwanted image of Ianthe Dimitriou rose in Harriet's mind.

'Sometimes he doesn't object,' she returned shortly, and went back to the car.

She found the place without difficulty. The ground floor of the house was being used as a pottery, although there was no one working there at present, and a flight of white stone stairs on the outside of the building led up to a shabby blue door.

She sat outside for a few moments, staring up at it as she marshaled her thoughts, deciding that to storm in, guns blazing, might not be the best policy after all. That a more reasoned approach might serve her better.

Accordingly, she went up the steps without hurrying, and tapped lightly on the door, dislodging a few more flakes of peeling paint in the process.

It was flung open at once, and Roan confronted her.

'Harriet?' His brows snapped together. 'What are you doing here? How did you find me?'

'Toula told me where you'd gone.' She hesitated. 'If this means that you're painting again, I'm glad.'

'And I am naturally honoured to please you.' His tone was ironic. 'Did you drive down here merely to encourage my endeavours, or is there some other reason?'

'I—needed to talk to you—away from the house, but if I'm interrupting something important...'

'No,' he said. 'Come in. I am simply clearing up a little after my long absence. Preparing to start again.'

He stood aside, and Harriet went in, breathing the familiar scents of wood, canvas and oils. There was little furniture—a trestle table at one side holding palettes and brushes, together with a bottle of ouzo and a glass, a couple of wooden chairs, and a battered couch like a chaise longue pushed against another wall. It was upholstered in cracked green leather, but in Ianthe's portrait it had been covered by a crimson velvet throw, Harriet remembered, trying not to look at it too closely.

'So,' Roan said. 'What can I do for you?'

She took a breath. 'I had lunch with your father today.'

'Ah,' he said. 'And he told you that your grandfather was expected here. So you wish to make sure the actor knows his lines.' His mouth twisted. 'Don't worry, Harriet *mou*. By the time Kyrios Flint joins us, I shall be word-perfect again.'

'No,' she said. 'It—it's not that.' She looked down at the dusty floor. 'He insisted on talking to me about us—about our marriage. It seems he's heard about our—our sleeping arrangements.'

Roan shrugged. 'What did you expect? Your habit of rumpling the other pillow each morning would not deceive a fly. And my father is a great believer in frankness.'

She flushed. 'Obviously. But he was quite impossible. My God, he practically told me to go home—and get on my back.'

'My poor Harriet, how unnerving for you.' Roan did not bother to hide his amusement. 'And how old-fashioned of him,' he added silkily. 'Perhaps you should have fought back. Told him there were other positions you preferred.'

For a moment, his dark eyes held a disturbingly reminiscent gleam, and Harriet looked hurriedly away. She said breathlessly, 'Well, I'd prefer to avoid any further distasteful conversations.' She took a breath. 'I hope you'll explain this to him. '

'And say what?' Roan enquired sardonically. 'The truth—that, apart from a few hours that are best forgotten, our marriage has been a total invention? Or shall I confess that our estrangement is my own doing, because I have come to prefer the charms of some girl in Athens?'

'And have you?' The words had escaped before she could stop them.

He shrugged. 'Why should you care?' He paused. 'But you are right—he should not have talked to you in such a way, and I will make that clear to him. Yet before you condemn him, please understand he spoke only from concern for me. And because of the pain my mother caused him all those years ago, which he still feels.'

'Yes,' she said. 'He mentioned—something about that. He said she broke his heart.'

'And he broke hers,' Roan said quietly. 'It was love at first sight for them both, but he expected her to be content to be nothing but his wife, and the mother of his children. But she was at the start of her career when they met, and she needed to paint as she needed air to breathe.

'She began to feel stifled, desperate, because she could not make him understand that she wanted more than domesticity and his money to spend, and in return he became hurt, then angry. Blamed her painting as the cause of their problems, and demanded she give it up.

'He would not compromise, and in the end there was such bitterness, so many quarrels, that she left him, taking me, his three-year-old son, with her to England.'

He walked over to the table, poured some ouzo into the glass, and offered it to her. When she declined it mutely, he tossed it down his throat, and poured some more, his face brooding.

'He was convinced she would soon realise they could not live apart from each other and go back to him,' he went on. 'Finally, he became impatient and tried to compel her return through me—by beginning a legal battle for custody, thinking this would force her hand.'

He sighed. 'After that, there was no hope of reconciliation. Just two people, who were once passionately in love, tearing each other to pieces through the courts. As a result, I hardly saw my father—he lost his temper and made some stupid threat to kidnap me—and when I did, it was always in England and under supervision.

'But I was allowed to write to him, and he to me, and in that way we came to know each other. And eventually, after some years, I was permitted to come to Greece and spend time with him.'

He drank some more ouzo. 'But always—always he asked about her. Was she well? Was she happy? Did I have photographs? And when she died, he mourned for her as if there had been no separation.'

He added almost wearily, 'He thought he could only show his love by keeping her close—making her share his dream instead of following her own. He has never understood that sometimes real love requires one to let the beloved go. Probably he never will.'

She said, 'That is—so sad.'

'But then the world can be a sad place.' He set down his empty glass. 'Now, have you anything further to discuss, or may I continue clearing up?'

She realised she was being dismissed, but she lingered. 'I—I could help.'

'Thank you,' he said. 'But no.' His ironic smile seemed to graze her skin. 'I can manage alone.'

'Yes,' Harriet said quietly. 'We can both do that.' She went past him, out into the dazzle of the harsh sunlight, and realised that she was shivering suddenly, as if she would never be warm again.

CHAPTER THIRTEEN

So, THIS was it, thought Harriet. The day that had been haunting her for months, turning her life upside down in the process, had finally arrived. Her twenty-fifth birthday.

And, so far, it seemed to be running true to form—an emotional rollercoaster ride, with no chance to jump free.

Beginning first thing that morning, when Roan, a towel draped round his hips, had walked out of their shared bathroom, totally without warning, and slid into bed beside her only heart-thudding seconds before Toula had knocked at the door with Harriet's tea.

It had also been a surprise, at a totally different level, to find that the tray Toula placed, beaming, on her night table was set with a pretty bone china teapot, patterned with briar roses, together with a matching cup, saucer and milk jug.

A present from the staff, Toula explained, in honour of the *kyria*'s birthday, and she departed, sending them a glance of twinkling approval over her shoulder.

'A reminder of England for you.' Roan threw back the covers, and left the bed, adjusting his towel as he did so. 'And their own idea.'

'How—lovely of them.' Harriet strove for normality, her pulses going wild. 'But it makes me feel such a fraud. You should have stopped them.'

'I doubt that I could.' He shrugged. 'They wish to show you goodwill, Harriet *mou*.' He glanced at her ironically. 'And when Toula tells how she found us in bed together, your stock will rise even higher.'

She stared at the briar roses. 'Isn't that setting a dangerous precedent?'

'No.' And as she glanced at him, taken aback by the bleakness of his response, he added, 'You had better get ready. My father and Kyrios Flint will be joining us for breakfast.'

She said, her voice subdued, 'I—I hadn't forgotten.' And watched him walk into the dressing room and close the door.

She lay still for a moment, conscious that she was missing that brief and unexpected warmth of him beside her. His longed-for nearness in a bed that, as she'd realised from the first, was very much smaller than the one they'd shared at the hotel, and not even as large as her own at the flat.

It was just an ordinary double bed, she thought, the sort that married couples all over the world occupied together. So what on earth was it doing here—unless, of course, Panayotis had mistaken Roan's instructions.

Or was it just another temporary measure for the duration of the marriage, and something he'd never had any intention of using himself?

Sighing, she finished her tea, and began to make her preparations for the day.

Her meeting with her grandfather the previous afternoon had not been the most promising of reunions, she reflected. Gregory Flint had arrived tired from the flight, and querulous with the heat.

'You look drawn, child,' he'd told her, standing back for a critical inspection after his initial embrace. 'Is anything the matter?'

Maybe I should wear a badge, Harriet thought, saying, *I am not pregnant.* She forced a smile. 'No, I'm fine—really.'

Dinner had proved a stilted affair. Prompted by her questions, Mr Flint had mentioned the company—'Young Audley's performance seems to be improving now he's out of your shadow.' The garden—'Not enough rain, and another damned hosepipe ban.' And Mrs Wade—'Thinks she's got arthritis, and keeps talking about retiring—moving near her sister in Cheltenham. I've told her the winters can be bad in Gloucestershire, and she won't like it.'

'You mean you won't like it.' Harriet had smiled at him, trying to coax him into a better mood. 'Because you'll have to train up someone new.'

He'd grunted. 'Perhaps it's time I considered making other changes, too.'

He had not, however, spoken directly about Gracemead, and not long after that Constantine Zandros had suggested courteously that his guest might appreciate an early night, and taken him away to the Villa Dionysius, leaving Harriet feeling oddly relieved on both counts.

However, she'd spent a restless night, and as she showered and dressed in a pale green skirt and a scooped-neck white top, she was aware of an indefinable sense of unease, as if a storm was gathering. Which was nonsense, because the sky was its usual untroubled blue.

Breakfast was served with champagne, and there were presents to be opened. Her grandfather had brought her the latest thing in digital cameras, but from Constantine Zandros she received a small framed watercolour of the beach below, with the initials 'VA' in the bottom right-hand corner.

She did not need Roan's quietly delighted, 'Papa...' to alert her to its significance. She looked at her father-in-law, and saw that the dark, autocratic face had softened, become almost wistful.

He said, 'Roan's mother left some paintings here, which I— kept. I thought you might like this scene that you know well. *Chronia pola!* Happy birthday.'

She said gently, 'It's a wonderful gift, and I shall treasure it always.' She smiled. *'Efharisto.'*

He inclined his head. *'Parakalo, pedhi mou.'*

Roan's present was in a long narrow box that could only mean jewellery. He did not consider, apparently, that her embargo applied to birthdays, she thought, bracing herself for the flash of diamonds as she opened the velvet case.

Instead, she found herself looking down at the exquisite simplicity of a plain gold cross and chain, and caught her breath.

Her eyes blurred as she lifted it from its satin bed. 'It's—so beautiful,' she told him huskily. 'It's absolutely perfect. Will you put it on for me?' And, as he hesitated, 'Please?'

She bent her head, thrilling to the remembered brush of his fingers against the nape of her neck as he fastened the little clasp, letting the cross settle at the base of her throat.

He said in a low voice, with a note in it she'd never heard before, 'May it protect you always, my Harriet.'

She looked down at the soft gleam of the gold, then turned to face him, lifting a shy hand to touch his cheek, and raising her mouth for his kiss, aware that his cool lips trembled a little as they took hers.

It had been such a long time, she thought, and found herself wishing urgently—desperately—that they were alone. That she could wind her arms round his neck and hold him close, so that their kiss could deepen to intimacy, and she'd feel his mouth exploring her neck, and the first swell of her breasts. That she could close her eyes, and forget everything in his arms.

But in reality he was already lifting his head, and stepping back, and the others were smiling and raising their glasses, Constantine with a certain irony, so the moment was over.

It doesn't matter, she thought. Whatever else the day brings, I can remember that, for an instant of time, I was truly happy.

When breakfast was over, however, Harriet discovered she was going to be left pretty much to her own devices. Constantine was whisking her grandfather away for a sightseeing tour of the peninsula, and the immediate hinterland, while Roan announced abruptly that he needed to return briefly to Athens, adding that he would be back in plenty of time for the evening celebration.

It was on the tip of her tongue to ask if she could go with him, but she simply nodded in acquiescence, and a while later she heard the helicopter depart.

Surplus to requirements all round, she thought, changing into her swimming gear, so she would spend the morning on the beach as usual. A day like any other day—and yet…

As she went down the steps, she wondered, not for the first time, why Roan had never joined here there, even when he was at home. He went down to swim, she knew, sometimes early in the morning, often last thing at night.

But never when I'm around, she thought bleakly. Maybe because he prefers to remember the bay when there was someone else to share it with him—someone passionate and uninhibited. Maybe he'd dispensed with the little table and chairs in that first painting because they were still reminders of past unhappiness.

She slipped off her wrap, straightening her shoulders, and flicking her hair back with restive fingers. To hell with the past—and her, she thought. I'm going for a swim.

The sand was already too hot to walk on, so she used the straw matting that was laid down each morning as a pathway to the sea. She waded in until she was waist deep, then turned into a crawl, setting herself the kind of lengths to cover she would find in a swimming pool.

Her serious exercise completed, she came back to the warm shallows, and spent a little time lying there, letting the water ripple over her, thinking almost idly as she did so what a paradise this would be for children, then realising with a pang that she couldn't afford to fantasise like that.

She'd blotted the water from her body, and was rubbing her hair with a towel, when she heard the sound of an outboard motor, and saw a dinghy coming round the headland, and heading towards the shore with two people on board.

Surprised, Harriet shaded her eyes to watch. Boats passed, of course, but this bay was strictly private property, she thought, and no one ever landed uninvited.

But today's visitors seemed oblivious to that, and she realised reluctantly that she'd have to be polite but firm with them.

As the dinghy neared the beach, the engine cut out, and a man wearing shorts and a checked shirt jumped into the water and began to drag it up on to the sand. Then he turned to help his passenger, who climbed out and stood for a moment, adjusting her filmy violet pareu, her cropped hair glittering like silver in the sunlight.

And suddenly Harriet realised just who this newcomer was—this unexpected and unwelcome intruder, swaying up the beach as if she was parading along a catwalk.

'*Kalimera.*' Under the pareu, she was wearing nothing but a thong, and her body gleamed as if it had been oiled. She looked Harriet up and down, her gaze mocking as she studied the demure lines of the chainstore bikini she was wearing. 'So you are the girl Roan brought from England as his wife. A choice, it seems, he now regrets.'

'And you are Ianthe Dimitriou,' Harriet returned pleasantly. 'Forgive me. I hardly recognised you with your clothes on.'

'That is English humour, *ne*?' The other shrugged, her breasts jutting under their thin veiling. 'It does not amuse me.'

'Good,' said Harriet, briskly. 'Then we have no need to prolong our acquaintance. Perhaps you'd tell your friend to take you back where you came from.'

'Friend?' Ianthe echoed incredulously. 'He works for Maria Chrysidas, at whose house I stay. He drives a boat. He is no one. And I am here only to get back my portrait that Roan painted. Now he has achieved success, it could be valuable, and I want it. So it is up to you when I leave.'

'I'm afraid you're out of luck.' Harriet tossed her towel on the lounger, and reached casually for her sunblock. 'Because your asset went up in smoke the day I arrived.'

'What are you saying?'

'That Roan had it put on a bonfire, along with the bedding your accomplice ruined.'

For a moment, Ianthe looked almost murderous, then she gave a harsh laugh. 'Well, if it is gone, so be it. It achieved much that I had hoped for. Your husband was reminded of all that he had lost, while you—you slapped his face and refused him your body.'

She clicked her tongue. 'The act of a fool, *kyria*. You think he will ever forget such insults? In spite of his mother's blood, he is a Greek, not a pallid Englishman who allows a woman to rule him.

'Already, he is planning to be rid of you, and find a wife more to his taste, and the whole world knows this and pities you. So why wait until you are told to leave. Why not—just go?'

'With you waiting in the wings to take my place, I suppose?' Harriet said scornfully.

'No,' the other girl said slowly, her mouth tightening into a hard line.

'That will not happen. As soon as I walked away from him, I knew that it was finished. That he would never look at me again.

Because that is the way of the Zandros men.' Her eyes blazed. 'You think I did not try?'

She added with sour triumph, 'And you will be forgotten also, as if you never existed, when he sends you away, back to your own country.'

Harriet threw back her head. She said coldly and clearly, 'I am Mrs Roan Zandros, and *this* is my country.' The words seemed to come out of nowhere, but they burned with a conviction that stunned her. 'Now, get out of here, before I call my staff and have you removed.'

'Brave words, *kyria*.' Ianthe shrugged again. 'But you will be weeping soon, and then you will remember that I told you so.'

Harriet waited, unmoving, until the dinghy was out of sight, then she sank down on to the nearest lounger, wrapping her arms round her body.

'I can expect nothing from you as my wife.' His words. And, even more damningly, *'Then there is no more to be said.'*

Is that what he'd meant—that he was drawing a line under something that was finished and turning away? *'The way of the Zandros men.'* Because everything he'd said and done over the past days seemed to confirm it.

Those brief minutes in bed with her this morning had set no precedent, because he knew she would not be here. Because in his own mind she had already gone.

'I can manage alone.'

But I can't, she cried out in silent anguish. I need him. I love him. I can't live without him.

Yet she might have to. This was what she now had to face. That she might have alienated him to such a degree that there was no way back for her.

And, if so, she knew that she had brought this on herself, by stubbornly refusing to accept the truth that her heart was telling her. That she'd seen him and wanted him, and everything else in her universe paled into insignificance beside that.

Even, she realised, Gracemead.

I used the house, she thought, as a barrier to keep him away because I was scared of what I felt for him. Because I dared not focus on my real feelings and how they were shifting. And, because of my mother's life, it was safer to love a pile of stones in the country than a living, breathing man who might break my heart. I thought I could not take the risk.

But that day at Tessa's I knew—I saw so very clearly what I wanted my life to be—yet even when I knew the truth about Lucy, and there was nothing to keep us apart—still—still I went on fighting. Fighting myself, and pretending that I was at war with him.

And now it could be too late. *Too late.*

She touched the cross at her throat. *'May it protect you always, my Harriet.'*

I didn't know it, she thought, but he was really saying goodbye. And so much for my moment of happiness.

Back at the house, she went in search of Panayotis.

'I need to talk to Kyrios Roan.' She forced a smile. 'Has he left any contact numbers with you, please? I—I forgot to ask him earlier.'

'He was to visit the office of his lawyer, *kyria*, but by now I think he will have left. Do you wish me to enquire?'

His lawyer... So, the process of separation had already begun, she thought, her heart dead and heavy, like a stone in her chest. He'd wasted no time. But why should he? He wanted this—hiatus in his life dealt with so that he could plan his future. He'd told her he was tired of pretending, so it was the practical thing to do.

'No,' she said with an effort. 'I think, after all, I'll wait.'

She would not beg. That was the only real conclusion she arrived at in the course of the longest day she'd ever spent.

When he told her his decision, she would accept it without a murmur. If nothing else, she would make sure their parting was dignified. No tears, no scenes, or useless recriminations. The last great pretence.

And whatever his lawyers offered her, she would refuse.

But she couldn't altogether figure what she'd be going back to. Her flat was let for a minimum of six months, and it was clear there'd be nothing for her at Flint Audley.

Perhaps, if Mrs Wade does call it a day, Gramps will take me on as housekeeper, she thought, with a sigh. Not that I'll be much good.

Maybe, instead of sunbathing, I should have asked Takis to teach me to cook. Got Panayotis to show me how the house was run. Then I'd be worth a living wage.

But I kept aloof from all that quite deliberately. I couldn't afford to become too attached to anything here—or anyone. To involve myself too closely. But somehow, without my knowing, this place got under my skin.

So that when I've been at my loneliest and most confused, I've found something in the rocks, the earth, and this eternal sky that's comforted me, and given me hope.

And when I go away, I shall be leaving hope behind.

Outwardly, she got on with her life—preparing for her birthday dinner with apparent tranquillity. She washed her hair, gave herself a manicure, and applied a face pack which made Toula squeak with alarm when she saw it—all the things she used to despise as unnecessary pandering to male appetites.

Now, she knew she owed it to herself. She would never be beautiful, but if this was to be her last evening as Roan's wife, she would make sure she looked as good as possible.

She chose a dress in white silk chiffon, low-cut, with narrow straps, and a full floating skirt. A dress for romance, she thought, and for a woman who expected—and wanted—to be undressed by her lover. And felt a sob rise in her throat.

But when he joined her on the terrace, lithe and heart-stoppingly glamorous in the formality of dinner jacket and black tie, she awarded him a cool smile as she sat, an untouched glass of wine in front of her.

'Is it time to go?'

'Presently.' Roan took a chair opposite, setting his glass of ouzo on the table. 'Panayotis tells me you wished to speak to me today.'

She'd hoped it wouldn't be mentioned. Fortunately, she could improvise, and she shrugged. 'I thought you should know that a friend of yours paid us a visit today.'

He frowned, not even bothering to query the caller's identity. 'Here—at the house? I was not told.'

'Down at the beach. She wanted her portrait back. I explained it wasn't possible, and she seemed a little miffed. Maybe you should offer to paint her again.'

'And maybe I would rather lose my hair, and half my teeth.' He studied her for a moment. 'Were you upset?'

'Dazzled,' she said promptly. 'It was like seeing that picture in action replay. I imagine the boatman who brought her found it difficult to keep his hand on the tiller.'

He gave a reluctant grin. 'But it was not for you to deal with her. I should have been here—for all kinds of reasons.' He paused. 'Unfortunately, my business in Athens was urgent.' He drank some ouzo, watching her reflectively. 'And also something that we need to discuss.'

A fist seemed to clench round her heart. She said swiftly, 'But not now—please. Can't it wait—until the party's over?'

'I thought you didn't want a party.'

'Like so much else, I've got used to the idea.'

'As you wish. But our talk is not something that can be postponed indefinitely.'

'I'm not trying to be evasive. Just to enjoy what's left of my birthday.' She hesitated. 'It was kind of your father to give me that picture. Especially when he disapproves of me so much.'

'It is our marriage he deplores, Harriet *mou*. He has criticised me too, believe me.'

She didn't look at him. 'Does he know about your girl in Athens?'

'No,' he said softly. 'Nor about the girl in Paris, the girl in New York or the girl in London. Is that what you wanted to hear?'

'It—really doesn't concern me. You're a free man.' Her throat tightened. 'And, with that in mind, perhaps we should talk now, after all.' She made herself meet his gaze. 'When are you sending me back to England?'

There was a heartbeat's pause, then he said, 'Tomorrow, with your grandfather. That—seems best.'

'Oh, it does,' she said. 'Quick and final, and no messing. Will I have time to pack?'

'The maids are doing it for you now.'

'My God,' she said huskily. 'Planned to the last detail. You really—can't wait.'

His own voice was harsh. 'There is nothing to wait for. This comedy we've been playing is finished, Harriet. It has fooled no one. Not my father, and certainly not your grandfather. He knew from the first that you did not wish to be my wife—that it was simply a means to an end. I think he blamed himself for having driven you to such lengths.'

'But he didn't stop me.'

'No,' he said. 'But he understands that it is time to put the whole sorry episode behind us and begin to live our own lives again.' He paused. 'It will be explained that you are going home to sign some legal documents.'

'Only I won't be coming back.' She picked up her wine glass, spilling a little because her hand was shaking, and drank. 'Are you planning to divorce me for desertion—history repeating itself?'

'We have a pre-nuptial agreement,' he said. 'Which provides for the ending of the marriage. Perhaps we should use it.'

'Of course,' she said. 'Why didn't I think of that? But, then, you must know it by heart—every loophole—every Freudian slip. I suppose you've had the divorce papers drawn up in advance—and they'll be the documents I'm going to sign.'

'No,' he said. 'That is a different matter, entirely. You see, your grandfather has decided, after all, to transfer Gracemead into your name, Harriet *mou*. In spite of everything, I think he was impressed with your ingenuity—and your single-minded determination.

'So, he will announce this special gift at dinner tonight—the evening of your twenty-fifth birthday. Which means that you have won. The house is yours, and your dream has come true at last.'

Only to turn, she thought, into a living nightmare. And all of her own making.

And she would have to smile and pretend to be delighted, when all she wanted to do was hide herself in some dark corner, and weep until she had no tears left to shed.

CHAPTER FOURTEEN

It WAS nearly three a.m. when Yanni drove Harriet back to the house. Roan did not accompany her, as many of the guests at the Villa Dionysius still showed no sign of leaving, but she couldn't take any more.

Dead on my feet, she thought wryly, and dying inside.

The 'dinner for a few friends' had not turned out at all as she'd expected. Constantine Zandros had simply reverted to Plan A, and buffet tables, sagging under the weight of the food, had been set on the lantern-hung terrace, to feed everyone within a hundred mile radius.

Or that was how it seemed, Harriet had thought, almost reeling back from the jovial roar of laughter and talk that assailed her from all sides from the milling crowd. On top of which, a group of musicians were trying valiantly to make themselves heard, and succeeding well enough for impromptu and vigorous dancing to break out at intervals.

All this when she wanted to disappear into a black hole, and never be found again. When she could have moaned aloud in pain and disbelief at what was happening to her.

Everyone wished to meet her, and her facial muscles were soon aching as badly as her heart from the need to smile and say *kalispera* as Roan escorted her from group to group, his hand inexorably cupping her elbow. Harriet could see the approving smiles following them, observing the tall young man so solicitous for his shy wife, so concerned for her comfort.

'This is such hypocrisy,' she muttered fiercely at one point.

'But they don't know that,' he returned unsmilingly. 'Look on it as a rite of passage before you regain your freedom. One last ordeal to be endured.'

Before the real one begins, she thought. The ordeal of the rest of my life without you. Oh, God—what am I going to do?

As the evening progressed, Harriet was approached by a steady stream of immaculately garbed, grey-haired men, all wishing to tell her in careful English that it was a matter of rejoicing for them all that their friend Constantine Zandros had been reunited with his son after so many bitter years, and such a fine boy too, so capable—so far-sighted.

But—*po po po*—the only son of an only son, which was to be regretted. Her duty made clear, accompanied invariably by a kindly smile.

And what am I supposed to say in reply? Harriet wondered wearily. That I'm an only child too, but the girl who'll be taking my place very soon will probably be a one-woman fertility fest?

She noticed at one point that Roan had been waylaid by a smartly dressed but clearly agitated brunette, her face imploring, and her crimson-tipped hands gesturing wildly as she talked.

But then she was aware of everyone he spoke to, she acknowledged wryly, her eyes endlessly scanning the crowd, looking for him, longing for him. And maybe it would be easier when Europe divided them, and such searching became pointless.

'Maria Chrysidas,' he told Harriet laconically, as he rejoined her, indicating that he must have seen her watching. 'Apparently her husband, who does business with me sometimes, overheard Ianthe bragging about this morning's escapade, and she has now left their house, never to return.'

'A move to turn her into a pariah?' she queried tautly.

'Not by me. I cannot speak for her own efforts.' He nodded towards a line of laughing people weaving their way along the terrace in a series of swirling, intricate steps. 'Come and dance with me.'

She hung back, wondering how much more togetherness she would be able to bear before she cracked. That having him near was almost more torture than when they were apart. 'No—thank you.' Adding hastily, 'I—I don't know how.'

'Then learn,' he said sardonically. 'Before conclusions are drawn, and every married woman here rushes over to advise you on morning sickness.'

'Perhaps you'd like to make an announcement,' she flung back at him. 'Making it clear that the future of the Zandros dynasty does not depend on me.'

'I don't need to say anything. It will become apparent soon enough.' He took her hand, pulling her into the dance. 'Now, listen to the rhythm, and watch the woman in yellow. She's good.'

At first she stumbled along, but gradually, with Roan's guidance, she began to pick up the pattern of the movements, and when the dance ended she was given a round of delighted applause.

Star of the show tonight, she thought with irony. An outcast like Ianthe tomorrow.

After that, she found herself dancing constantly, but never again with Roan.

However, the highspot of the evening came when Gregory Flint rose to announce the real birthday present he was giving his granddaughter—the English country house known as Gracemead—and Harriet heard a loud murmur of pleased surprise ripple through the crowd, as his words were translated and passed back.

She stood beside him as he hugged her awkwardly, always a little embarrassed by any public show of affection, and did her best to look grateful, delighted, thrilled, instead of sick at heart, and frightened. As she tried to remember that this was what she'd always wanted, so how could it possibly matter so little—be a burden instead of a joy?

Nobody watching would ever understand why she should see her good fortune as a defeat, and not a victory.

Becoming an instant heiress, she realised, had probably doubled if not trebled her approval rating, and made her almost worthy of her status as a Zandros wife.

She was soon surrounded by some of the younger women she'd met before, all still eager to know when she would visit their houses—have lunch—go shopping—and saw their disappointment as she explained that she had to go back to England, that there were formalities about her wonderful house to attend to, and, yes, she was so lucky—so happy—because it was the best birthday gift in the world—a dream come true.

And saw Roan watching her from the other side of the terrace, his eyes shadowed, his face expressionless.

Her bedroom was cheerless with all those half-packed suitcases lining the walls.

She'd pleaded tiredness in order to excuse herself, but she knew she wouldn't sleep for what little was left of the night.

And recalled painfully all those other nights, when she'd lain there in that bed, sleepless with loneliness, never guessing that Roan was also awake elsewhere—but for very different reasons.

How casually he'd told her about his other night companions, she thought bitterly, as she struggled out of her dress and tossed it, unfolded, into the nearest case. Assuming, she supposed, that she wouldn't care, when even the thought of him making love to anyone else tore her emotions to ribbons of blood.

I turned him back into a single man, she thought wretchedly. Now I have to live with the consequences.

And it meant that she was once again a single woman. 'Hell's spinster' as Jon Audley had once cruelly described her. Her future as barren as her body, because the life she was returning to—had thought she wanted—was no life at all.

She slipped off her scraps of underwear, and put on her robe, a classic style in heavy silk, the colour of amethysts, and the only garment that Roan had bought for her before they left London.

She'd been faintly embarrassed when she'd found the beribboned box on her bed, but there'd been nothing about the contents that she could object to. On the contrary, it was beautiful, so she'd offered him a stilted word of thanks, and worn it.

She fastened the sash in a bow around her slender waist, then quietly slid open the glass doors, and stepped out barefoot on to the terrace that surrounded the house.

She sat down on one of the cushioned chairs, and leaned back, staring into the warm darkness. It was very still. Even the cicadas were silent, while, across at the Villa Dionysius, the music had stopped, and she could see the rake of car headlights as the last guests finally departed. The party was over, and Roan would be coming back.

I shouldn't be out here, she told herself restively. I should be indoors, in bed, pretending to be asleep. Not hanging round as if I was waiting for one last glimpse of him. Hoping for something he can't give me.

How pathetic, she thought, that here she was, twenty-five years old, sighing for a man who'd once spent the night with her because it was his right to do so. Who'd taught her unforgettably about passion, but left her to discover love for herself. And who'd decided she had no further part to play in his life.

And how ironic that the people she'd met that evening had been so readily prepared to accept her as Roan's wife, when the three people closest to her couldn't wait for the marriage to end.

Yes, she'd struggled with the hints about providing him with an heir. But maybe she wouldn't have minded so much if having his baby had been a real possibility. She might even have shared their comments with him later, as she went, laughing, into his arms.

Instead, it was another sadness she would take with her when she left. And Gracemead, the house her grandfather had always insisted was a home for families, would only compound the hurt. The sense of isolation.

She straightened her shoulders defensively. But her return would not be all unhappiness, she reminded herself. There was Tessa's baby to look forward to, and, if she was to be denied children of her own, she would make sure she was the world's best godmother.

'Harriet.'

She started at the sound of her name, realising she'd been totally unaware of his approach. Yet there he was, standing in front of her, tie unfastened, and carrying his shoes.

'What are you doing out here?'

'I could ask you the same thing,' she returned defensively. 'I didn't expect you to be creeping around the garden.'

'I decided to walk back along the beach. But you have a journey tomorrow. You should be asleep.'

I have years and years to sleep, she thought, but only such a little while to stay awake with you.

She shrugged. 'I can rest on the plane.' She paused. 'It was lucky you could get me a ticket at such short notice.'

'We are part-owners of the airline,' he said. 'It helps.'

'Ah, yes,' she said. 'I was forgetting. One snap of your fingers, and people rush to do your bidding.'

His voice was dry. 'I never found you particularly biddable, Harriet *mou*.' He moved across the terrace towards the glass doors.

She said jerkily, 'Roan—don't go. Not yet.'

His voice was quiet. 'I have to work tomorrow.'

'Of course.' She bent her head. 'Just—another busy day.'

He hesitated. 'Did you want something in particular?'

Yes, she thought, I—I want you, and if it was just a question of crossing this terrace to reach you, then I'd do it. But there've been too many harsh words—too many rejections—and you've gone far—far away. Too far.

She said haltingly, 'There might still be—things to say.'

'If it is a question of money,' he said, 'you will find me generous.' He smiled faintly. 'More so than you were prepared to be with me.'

'No,' she said, gasping. 'Oh, God, no. I—I won't take a penny. I have contacts with a couple of firms of head-hunters in the UK, and I intend to work.'

He was silent for a moment, then he said courteously, 'Allow me to wish you every success. *Kallinichta*.'

She followed him into the lamplit bedroom. Do something, she thought. Take a risk. After all, he's a gambler, and he might understand.

She caught at his sleeve. 'I don't want to be alone.' Her voice was small, husky. 'Not tonight. Stay with me—please.'

He looked at the bed, and then at her, his mouth twisting, as she fumbled with the sash of her robe, trying to unfasten the bow.

He said quite gently, 'You don't know what you are asking, Harriet. And the answer is—no.'

Her hands stilled. 'You don't want me?'

'No doubt I could do so.' He lifted a shoulder in an infinitesimal shrug. 'But I have discovered that wanting is not enough. So—goodnight.'

His door closed behind him. That would be her abiding memory of her time here, she thought, numbly. Doors closing—shutting her out.

And, now, none of them would ever open for her again.

'Well, that's that,' Gregory Flint said briskly. 'And everything has finally turned out for the best.' He patted her hand. 'Don't look so wan, my dear. You'll soon be home where you belong, and you can put all this nonsense behind you.'

Harriet, who'd been staring dully out of the car window, roused herself, and nodded dutifully.

She said, 'Grandfather, I'm really sorry for what I did. It was—unspeakably stupid.'

'You're not entirely to blame, my child. I assumed that you'd be seeing people—young men—and if it was simply a question of making your mind up, all you needed was—a gentle push in the right direction.'

A gentle push? thought Harriet. My God, it was like being rammed amidships.

'I never thought you would deliberately pick a complete stranger. And was quite stunned when he came to see me, and told me what was going on.' He snorted. 'And he had the nerve to beat me at chess, arrogant young devil. Well, he's not so sure of himself now, in spite of his millions, and his damned charm.'

'Did he beat you?' Harriet frowned. 'He told me it had ended in stalemate.'

'Ah,' he said. 'That was another matter entirely.'

She was silent for a moment. 'Gramps, if you—knew, why didn't you say something—put a stop to it?'

'I should have done, but I had this irresistible desire to see your would-be husband fall flat on his face. Well, he can't say he wasn't warned. And he's behaved decently enough, I suppose, for someone who hasn't had many failures in life—especially with women.'

'Warned—about what? I don't understand.'

'About you, my dear, and Gracemead. I told him he wouldn't win.

That nothing and no one in this world would ever matter to you as much as that house. But he didn't believe me. Said that, although you did not love him yet, that would change when you were married, because he loved you so much that he knew he could persuade you to care for him in return.

'He was actually convinced that he could make you forget Gracemead, and choose to spend your life with him instead.'

'He—said that?' Harriet hardly recognised her own voice.

'With a lot of other nonsense about protecting you, and wanting to devote his life to your happiness. Sheer self-delusion, and I told him so. But I offered him a sporting chance. Told him he had until your birthday to win you over.

'I wasn't best pleased when he whisked you over to Greece, but I made it clear the deadline stood. That all I'd have to do was dangle the house in front of you, and you'd be off back to England in spite of his money.'

He looked at her with an air of satisfaction. 'And here we are. I knew you wouldn't let me down, bless you.'

She said numbly, 'He loved me and he could let me go—just like that?'

Mr Flint stirred uncomfortably. 'Give him his due, he didn't want to, in spite of his father's urging. Begged me for more time, which I guarantee he doesn't do every day. Even tried to call off the deal altogether. In the end, I had to tell him that unless he kept his word to set you free, I'd sell Gracemead over your head, and see if you'd still want to love him after that.'

He added, 'And that, naturally, was the clincher.'

'Yes,' she said. 'I can see that it—might be.' She took a deep breath. 'Oh, God, what's the Greek for—Turn the car round?' She leaned forward, tapping the driver's shoulder. 'Yanni—stop.' She gestured frantically. 'Go back—back to Militos. To Kyrios Roan. I swear I'll start language lessons tomorrow if you'll just understand me now.'

'Harriet,' her grandfather said sternly. 'Are you out of your mind?'

'No,' she said. 'Just the opposite. Oh, thank heavens,' she added, as Yanni, muttering, turned the car in the opposite direction. 'Now—hurry.'

'I wasn't joking.' Gregory Flint's tone was grim. 'Unless you come home with me now, I shall indeed sell the house. I've had several good offers.'

'Then take one of them. Take them all, if you want. I don't care any more.' Her voice cracked. 'The only home I want is here, with my husband, and somehow I have to make him believe that.'

When they reached the house, Harriet was out of the car almost before it had stopped. She flew into the house, calling Roan's name, running into the *saloni*, but the figure standing by the window was her father-in-law, and she halted, gasping with disappointment.

'Harriet.' Constantine Zandros gave her a long look. 'I thought we had seen the last of you. What have you done with your grandfather?'

'He's in the car, and I'm sure you hoped you were rid of me.' She lifted her chin, glaring at him. 'But you're going to be disappointed, Kyrios Zandros. I'm back to stay, and there's not a damned thing you can do about it.'

She swallowed. 'I'm your son's wife, and I'll camp on the doorstep if I have to until he takes me back. Because I love him—do you hear me?' She almost sobbed the words. 'Oh, God, I love him more than anything in the world, and I'm going to tell him so.'

His glance went past her. He said dryly, 'I think, my child, that he already knows.'

Harriet whirled round, and saw Roan standing in the doorway behind her. He was dressed for travel in a business suit, carrying a briefcase, and he was staring at her, his dark face haggard, blank with shock. For a moment, he did not move or speak, then he said hoarsely, 'Is it true?'

'Yes,' she said passionately. 'Yes, it is. I was just too stupid to realise it at first, and then I was too scared to say it. Because you were always walking away.'

'I did not trust myself to stay,' he said. 'Not if you did not love me.'

'But you loved me,' she said. 'Enough to let me go, so that I could have my dream.' She looked at him, her heart in her eyes. 'Oh, darling, how could you think I would ever want a pile of stones in the country more than you?'

Constantine Zandros cleared his throat. 'I think I shall find Kyrios

Flint,' he remarked to the room at large. 'Attend to his comfort. I will see you both later. Perhaps in a few days.' He smiled at Harriet quite gently. 'Maybe then, *pedhi mou*, you may feel able to call me Papa.'

And he went, leaving them together.

Roan took a step towards her, and she flung up a hand, halting him. She said quickly, the words falling over themselves, 'Darling, there's something I've got to say, before I—we…' She gave a little gasp. 'I—I don't blame you for anything you've done, because I've been such a bitch, and you must have been so lonely. But I can't—share you. Not if we have a real marriage. It would destroy me.'

'Ah,' he said reflectively. 'My girl in Athens and everywhere else.' He took out his wallet and extracted a piece of paper, folded small. 'You may recognise her.'

It was a sheet from a sketch block. A drawing of someone, lying in bed, the coverlet drawn loosely over her hips. Her head was resting on her arm, her hair a cloud on the pillow. Her face was softened, beautiful, and she was smiling in her sleep.

She said huskily, 'When did you do this?'

'After our wedding night. I woke early, and all I could think of was your voice telling me you would never love me. I was so scared it might be true, and I needed a talisman to keep with me—to give me hope. It has been my salvation.'

She glanced at the drawing again. She said shyly, 'I don't—really look like this.'

'You did,' he said gently. 'And you will again. Each morning of our lives, my sweet one.'

Her lips trembled into a smile. 'You can't call me that. I'm not remotely sweet.'

'You are to me.' The look in his eyes brought the colour to her face. 'My sweet, lost, lonely, difficult love.'

'All the times I told you I didn't want you,' she whispered. 'I'll make them up to you, I swear it.'

'I am delighted to hear it.' He came to her, lifting her into his arms, and carrying her down the passage towards their bedroom. 'Perhaps you should start now while this repentant mood lasts.'

He undressed her slowly, and with immense care, as if he was unwrapping a precious treasure. Smiled into her enraptured eyes as he took her, as he moved with her in deepening intensity until, at the last, all control deserted them both and the searing delight of their mutual rapture brought a healing beyond all words.

A long time later, she said dreamily, 'This is such a wonderful bed. You're always within my reach.'

'At last a plan that works.' His lips were against her hair, his hands beginning a new adventure. 'But I think we will have to spend some time in other beds, *agapi mou*. I want to take you on honeymoon.'

'Mmm.' She tried a few enticements of her own. 'Anywhere in particular, *kyrie*?'

He hesitated, his face suddenly serious. 'I thought—South America. That is why I saw my lawyers in Athens yesterday. They think their enquiry agents may have traced your mother.'

For a long moment, she could not speak. 'You—you've done all that—for me? Oh, my love.' She paused, swallowing back her tears. 'You do realise she may not want to see me, after all this time.'

'I think she will,' he said. 'But we will find out together.'

'Yes,' Harriet said with a sigh of pure happiness. 'Together.' And lifted her mouth to his.

HARLEQUIN®

Mediterranean NIGHTS™

Sometimes you need someone to teach you the things you already know....

Coming in February 2008

CABIN FEVER

by

Mary Leo

Vacationing aboard *Alexandra's Dream* with her two kids and her demanding mother-in-law, widow Becky Montgomery is not about to start exploring love again. But when she meets Dylan Langstaff, the ship's diving instructor, she realizes she might be ready to take the plunge....

Available wherever books are sold starting the second week of February.

HM38968

HARLEQUIN Presents

THE ROYAL HOUSE OF NIROLI

Always passionate, always proud.

**The richest royal family in the world—
a family united by blood and passion,
torn apart by deceit and desire.**

By royal decree Harlequin Presents is delighted to bring you
The Royal House of Niroli. Step into the glamorous, enticing
world of the Nirolian Royal Family. As the king ails he must
find an heir.… Each month an exciting new installment
follows the epic search for the true Nirolian king. Eight heirs,
eight passionate romances, eight fantastic stories!

A ROYAL BRIDE
AT THE SHEIKH'S
COMMAND
by Penny Jordan
Book #2699

A desert prince makes his claim to the
Niroli crown.… But to Natalia Carini
Sheikh Kadir is an invader—he's already
taken Niroli, now he's demanding her
as his bride!

www.eHarlequin.com   HP12699

REQUEST YOUR FREE BOOKS!

 HARLEQUIN *Presents* ®

PASSION GUARANTEED SEDUCTION

2 FREE NOVELS
PLUS 2
FREE GIFTS!

YES! Please send me 2 FREE Harlequin Presents® novels and my 2 FREE gifts. After receiving them, if I don't wish to receive any more books, I can return the shipping statement marked "cancel." If I don't cancel, I will receive 6 brand-new novels every month and be billed just $3.80 per book in the U.S., or $4.47 per book in Canada, plus 25¢ shipping and handling per book and applicable taxes, if any*. That's a savings of close to 15% off the cover price! I understand that accepting the 2 free books and gifts places me under no obligation to buy anything. I can always return a shipment and cancel at any time. Even if I never buy another book from Harlequin, the two free books and gifts are mine to keep forever.

106 HDN EEXK 306 HDN EEXV

Name	(PLEASE PRINT)
Address	Apt. #
City	State/Prov.	Zip/Postal Code

Signature (if under 18, a parent or guardian must sign)

Mail to the **Harlequin Reader Service**®:
IN U.S.A.: P.O. Box 1867, Buffalo, NY 14240-1867
IN CANADA: P.O. Box 609, Fort Erie, Ontario L2A 5X3

Not valid to current Harlequin Presents subscribers.

Want to try two free books from another line?
Call 1-800-873-8635 or visit www.morefreebooks.com.

* Terms and prices subject to change without notice. NY residents add applicable sales tax. Canadian residents will be charged applicable provincial taxes and GST. This offer is limited to one order per household. All orders subject to approval. Credit or debit balances in a customer's account(s) may be offset by any other outstanding balance owed by or to the customer. Please allow 4 to 6 weeks for delivery.

Your Privacy: Harlequin is committed to protecting your privacy. Our Privacy Policy is available online at www.eHarlequin.com or upon request from the Reader Service. From time to time we make our lists of customers available to reputable firms who may have a product or service of interest to you. If you would prefer we not share your name and address, please check here. ☐

HP07

Inside ROMANCE

Stay up-to-date on all your romance reading news!

Inside Romance is a FREE quarterly newsletter highlighting our upcoming series releases and promotions.

Visit

www.eHarlequin.com/InsideRomance

to sign up to receive our complimentary newsletter today!

IRN11107

HARLEQUIN Presents

**Harlequin Presents would like
to introduce brand-new author**

Christina Hollis

and her fabulous debut novel—

ONE NIGHT IN HIS BED!

Sienna, penniless and widowed, has caught the eye
of the one man who can save her—Italian tycoon
Garett Lazlo. But Sienna must give herself to him
totally, for one night of unsurpassable passion....

Book #2706

*Look out for more titles by Christina, coming soon—
only from Harlequin Presents!*

www.eHarlequin.com

HP12706